C000141215

Evensong

By Hugh Morrison

MONTPELIER PUBLISHING
2024

Published in Great Britain by Montpelier Publishing.
www.hughmorrisonbooks.com
Set in Palatino Linotype 10.5 point
Cover image by Miguna Studio
ISBN: 9798322956075

Follow Montpelier Publishing on Facebook

Chapter One

The Reverend Doctor Clement Layton Adams, a ruddy, squat man more like a farmer in appearance than a clergyman, sat on his favourite bench, tucked away on a shady corner of Cathedral Green. He lit a cigarette thoughtfully, gazing across the expanse of lawn to the medieval edifice which towered over the small Suffolk city of Midchester.

He inhaled deeply and flicked some imaginary ash from the end of his cigarette into the iron waste-paper bin beside him, then checked his watch to make sure he was not late for Evensong. He kept up his habit of a five minute rest on the bench in all but the most inclement weather; it was as much a part of his working day as the arrival of the tea trolley was to the office worker; it signified for him a winding down of duties and the gradual arrival of the end of the day.

It was mid-September; that time in England when the season hovers between summer and autumn, and seems for a week or so to be uncertain as to which of those it should turn. The day had been mild and sunny but the mist was beginning to gather, suggesting the arrival of a cool evening on which the less frugal residents of Midchester might consider lighting their fires.

For now, though, Adams had no need of his overcoat; his cassock providing ample warmth. He never smoked when wearing a surplice; he thought it unseemly and besides, there were practical considerations; a burn hole could ruin a good surplice.

He could, of course, have simply smoked in his study, and indeed he often did, but there he was likely to be disturbed by calls on his attention due to his position as Canon Chancellor, responsible for the Cathedral School and archives. Here, under the shade of a large yellowing sycamore tree, he was rarely disturbed. He reflected, as he often did, how lucky he was to work in such a place.

Midchester Cathedral bore a certain resemblance to Salisbury's, albeit with a shorter spire; so much so that it was sometimes called 'Salisbury's Sister' by antiquarians. Although there had been a church on the site since Saxon times, the present building dated largely from the fourteenth century and was built in the Early English style.

Adams had once heard an old forester say that every morning he worked in the same wood, but every morning he saw something new in it. It was the same for Adams; every evening when he sat for his contemplative cigarette, he saw something new in the cathedral.

It was no different today. His eyes travelled over the truncated spire at the top of the building, its tip catching the last rays of the sun, down to the graceful, high nave and the various other parts of the structure whose names will only be familiar to students of medieval architecture.

He looked at the Cathedral School, a square, Georgian building just opposite the cloisters; he saw the first choirboys begin to saunter along from there to Evensong, and checked his watch to make sure he was still in good time.

He was. He puffed on his cigarette, and then his gaze moved to the Cathedral Close adjacent to him, where the majority of the staff, including himself lived; it was, he

2

knew, one of the finest examples of an early Restoration terrace in the country, made even more beautiful with its view of the winding River Midwell and the flood-plain known as Midwell Meads beyond. Then, to his right, he saw an electric light flicker on in the saloon bar of the Duke of Norfolk, the large Tudor public house which marked the boundary between the Cathedral Green and the rest of Midchester. He looked at his watch; it was now just before six p.m; they would be getting ready for opening time.

He looked away from the secular building and turned his attention to the cathedral again. Such a beautiful place, he thought, as he always did. Except today, a darker thought was creeping into his mind, like a minor descent in a joyful piece of music. Was it possible he could lose all this, and all because of the actions of one man?

The trickle of choirboys in the cloisters had now become a stream, and the tenor bell in the tower began to toll. He heard the distant sound of the organ drift over the still air. He stubbed his cigarette out on the waste-paper basket and dropped it neatly inside, stood up and began to walk across the Green. Then he stopped. He realised what new thing he had seen today.

There was a figure standing in the shadows under one of the great buttresses by the south wall of the cathedral; clad in a light coloured mackintosh with its collar turned up and with a tweed cap pulled down low, obscuring any features.

Adams frowned. He had a nasty suspicion who it might be. He considered a confrontation, but thought better of it. He did not have time, and thought, darkly, that he might not be able to control himself. His bad temper was well known (the choirboys, he knew, called him Angry Adams) but lately, it seemed to have become worse and he did not trust himself not to create a scene.

Instead, he hurried into the cathedral just in time to don his surplice as the boys began to sing a William Byrd introit at the west door.

The Very Reverend Eckhart Tobias Devereux Vale, Dean of Midchester Cathedral, stood alone in the King's Gallery as Evensong began. It was his practice to do so when he was not leading the service, as it enabled him to have a bird's eye view of the proceedings, to be able to critically analyse and make mental notes on how it might be altered.

The timber gallery spanned the north transept, to the left of the high altar, at a height of some thirty feet, and had been constructed in 1814 for a royal visit which had never happened. It was reached by a wrought iron spiral staircase which was technically out of bounds to all but the most senior cathedral staff; a chain with a stern 'no entry' sign ensured no ordinary members of the public could disturb his private devotions.

Some, looking up at the Dean in the gallery, might think he had rather a royal bearing; indeed he came from the minor fringes of the aristocracy, and his elegant figure, aquiline features and fine head of greying hair were somewhat reminiscent of the young Prince Regent.

But that was as far as any monarchist resemblances went. For Vale was known by the popular press as the 'Red Dean' for his socialist views and for his ability to almost constantly create outrage, which sent the correspondence pages of the more conservative newspapers into a frenzy. Ecclesiastical controversies which had slumbered since the days of Darwin and Huxley, were suddenly big news

4

again, and the editors loved him for it.

In the eighteen months since his appointment, traditions had been hurled aside, sinecures had been revoked, icons (sometimes literally) had been torn down; funds allocated to independence movements in the colonies, and unemployed marchers had been allowed to camp in the cloisters. In short, the fervent atmosphere of progressivism had begun to pervade the ancient institution which he ruled over.

His latest 'stunt', as one journalist had described it, was the placing of the Red Flag and the flags of Sinn Fein and the Indian National Congress alongside the regimental banners which hung from the King's Gallery, an affront which had caused the leader of the local British Legion to resign in protest.

It had been rumoured that a group of undergraduates from Cambridge were planning to tear the flags down, which gave him another reason to sit in the King's Gallery whenever possible during services.

'Dearly beloved brethren...'

The clear voice of Dr Adams, the Canon Chancellor, rang out as he began to recite the opening prayer. Vale always found this an overly wordy and irksome piece of devotion, and made a mental note to have it cut in future. Although by law he was restricted in what he could add to the liturgy, there was very little to stop him simply cutting out the parts he did not like. Brevity was not only the soul of wit, he decided, but of religion also. Verbosity, in his view, was bourgeois.

He remained seated in the rush-seated chair in the gallery; there were no hassocks and anyway, he disapproved of kneeling to pray, considering it an outmoded remnant of medieval monarchism.

After what seemed like an age the opening prayers were

5

concluded, and the Canon Precentor, the leader of music, sang out in ringing tones the first *precis* of the service:

'O Lord open thou our lips…'

As the choir sang the response, 'And our mouth shall show forth thy praise,' Vale's attention was caught by a movement on the edge of his vision. The window of the south transept was clear glass. Much of it dated from the Georgian era and was uneven, giving a blurred view of the cathedral green beyond, but in the intervening years some panes had been replaced by modern glass.

He was therefore able to make out what the movement was; a figure in a raincoat and cap, walking quickly in an easterly direction. He felt a sudden stab of panic. Could it be…? He sighed with relief as he realised the figure was striding away from the main door, and so was unlikely to enter the cathedral.

The organ began to thunder, and Vale stood up as the office hymn began. He felt a slight wobble in his legs from fear. He wondered if his face had turned pale also, and was glad that he was standing where nobody was likely to notice.

'All done thank you George. You can wash him down now.'

Millicent Reynolds deftly swung her leg over the back of Bounder, her twelve year old dapple-grey gelding, and jumped down onto the cobbled stones of the stable-yard. She handed the reins over to the servant and removed her head-scarf, shaking her cropped blonde hair out. She cut a good figure in her riding clothes and, at 35, was still able to turn men's heads even when not on a horse.

'Had a good run, ma'am?' asked George Fletcher, his

gnarled hands soothing the horse's neck as it shook its head slightly, seemingly unwilling to be led away from its mistress into the stable.

'There now boy, it's only old George,' he said. 'Naught to worry about.'

'Yes, wonderful,' said Millicent. 'All the way across the Meads as far as the ford. Not bad for a middle-aged horse.'

'He's a good 'un, this,' said George knowingly. 'Lord knows why your father didn't put him to stud. He could have sired a few Grand National winners, him. I'll get him washed for yer.'

George touched the peak of his cap and led Bounder into the stable with a clatter of hooves.

Millicent silently wished her late father had indeed been able to spot the potential of the horse, now irrevocably lost. But then that had been Daddy all over, she thought. A hopeless old romantic with very little business sense, qualities he had passed on to his son and heir, Millicent's brother Tom.

When their father had died a few years previously it had become apparent that the family fortunes had been seriously depleted; death duties and the slump which began in 1929 had now reduced them to almost nothing.

She was glad, she reflected, that her mother, who had died before her father, had not lived to witness their reduction in circumstances. She had died in December 1914, before any of the real changes occurred. She had been despatched to the family vault in the grounds in full Victorian splendour, in that time before the King had discouraged the wearing of full mourning. It would have broken her heart to see the changes wrought by the war.

Millicent turned the corner from the small stable block to the gravel drive in front of Mead Lodge, her family home. The squat, ivy-covered building was a mishmash of Tudor,

Jacobean and Restoration architecture with a too-large and overly ornate neo-gothic conservatory tacked on the side, a relic of her grandfather's day, the last time the family had had any real money.

'Nights are drawing in something shocking, ma'am,' said George's wife Winnie as Millicent stepped into the hall, pausing to wipe her riding boots on the scraper by the door. Winnie, the last of the 'indoor' servants from the old days, took her riding mac and waited until she had removed her boots, then took them also.

'I'll put these away for you ma'am,' she said. 'Time was when we used the tack room for all this sort of thing, and no lady would have stepped through the front door in riding clothes. Your late mother, rest her soul, would have had the vapours. And *she* only rode side-saddle,' she added, with a hint of a disapproving glance. 'I daresay there'll be some supper for you presently, if Mr Fletcher's finished all his other jobs and can help me with it. I wanted to ask you, ma'am…'

'Yes, thank you Winnie,' interrupted Millicent quickly. 'Supper in the small drawing room would be lovely. Now I must go and wash'.

'Very good ma'am,' said Winnie, and trudged off to the servant's quarters at the back of the house, mumbling something indistinct under her breath.

She's getting worse, thought Millicent as she climbed the stairs to her bedroom. She had cut off the servant's chatter as she knew the woman was going to bring up the subject of money; there was always some bill or other that needed to be paid and many of them now were arriving with increasingly strident demands on them in red ink.

She stripped off her riding clothes and had a quick wash at the jug and bowl in the corner of her room; no sense wasting coke on the geyser for a hot bath. Then she dressed in an old but serviceable dark evening dress and began to brush her hair at the dressing table. It was absurd, she thought, and yet somehow comforting, to keep up the custom of dressing for dinner. Then she stopped, and tears began to prick at her eyes.

There was no getting away from it. She was going to have to give up Bounder, and then eventually, the house itself. The simple fact she had to face was that there were just no more economies that could be made. She could not turn out the Fletchers at their age; they had served her family nearly all their lives, and she knew that their pay was much less than it ought to be for a house this size, but they were fiercely loyal and would probably have worked for nothing if she had asked them. Having servants was bad enough, she thought, but having *unpaid* servants was unthinkable.

She had been hoping that now they were both well into their sixties they would have announced their retirement; she had even hinted at it, but no such luck; they would probably stay here until the bailiffs dragged them out and the whole place was knocked down or turned into a preparatory school.

She heard the gentle sound of the dinner gong, checked that her eye make-up was not affected by tears, and walked down the large staircase (oak, with carvings by a pupil of Grinling Gibbons). Nowadays, supper (it was too small a meal to call dinner) was served in the small drawing room, rather than the grander dining room, which lay for most of the year in shuttered darkness, its high-backed dining chairs shrouded in white dust-sheets as if a party of Georgian ghosts had gathered for a meal that would never end.

'I've a foo things to get on with if you don't mind, ma'am,' said Winnie as they met at the foot of the stairs.

9

'You'll manage by yourself I'm sure.'

'Thank you Winnie, I will manage on my own,' said Millicent. It was the same routine most nights; Winnie served up a frugal meal and then hurried off to do her 'foo things' somewhere else. Millicent suspected the woman was ashamed of the sparse food she was serving. Tonight it was cold mutton, with beans and potatoes from George's vegetable patch, and a jug of water. The wine cellar had run dry long since, and she could no longer afford to replenish it.

As she chewed the tough mutton she looked around at the room, a heavy depression settling on her. The dark, ornate Victorian furnishings with their thin layer of dust always made her feel like Miss Haversham. She glanced at the huge equestrian portrait of her husband, Captain the Honourable Francis Alois Reynolds, hurriedly painted in August 1914 before he had left for the front.

He looked sternly down on her as he always did, resplendent in his Household Cavalry dress uniform. Behind him was depicted an absurd pitched battle between British and German cavalry dressed in full regimentals, as if it were 1814 rather than a century later. She was quite certain no such battle had ever taken place, nor had he ever gone into combat on a horse.

They had met and married in the whirlwind of war when he was on leave in 1917, and three months later he was dead, killed ingloriously by a mudslide caused by a German artillery barrage near Arras. She was left an eighteeen-year-old widow, with just a small army pension; it turned out the Reynolds family had been almost as penniless as her own. Her brother Tom did his best, but he lived in a romantic world of his own, his small church stipend doing little to help.

She had had offers, of course; but most men of her age

and class had been killed in the war; she found younger men silly and irresponsible, and older ones full of stuffy ideas, unable to accept how things had changed. To marry simply because one needed money, in 1934, seemed to Millicent to be no better than...well, she wouldn't give such an occupation a name, even in her head.

As she finished her supper, she heard the clock bell of the cathedral, far away across the Meads. A guilty smile crept across her face, and she pushed back a lock of blonde hair as she caught sight of herself in the ancient dappled mirror across the room. There *might* be one way the family fortunes might be reversed. She had been thinking about it for some time. *Could* it be made to work?

It would mean scandal, of course, but that was in some sense what she craved. Her life of a pseudo-aristocratic countrywoman with its round of charity work and committees had begun to pall; it was a third of the way through the twentieth century and yet she felt as if she were trapped in the nineteenth. It was time, she decided, for Progress. It was happening on the continent now; why not here too?

She frowned as she remembered that lately she had received a setback to her plan. Was she simply building castles in the air? She decided to visit the Cathedral again to find out.

The Reverend Lucian Shaw, vicar of All Saints' church in the village of Lower Addenham, Suffolk, stepped off the train at Midchester station in the gathering dusk. He was immediately met by the porter who had brought his bicycle from the goods van. Shaw, who recognised the employee by sight, thanked him and passed him sixpence, receiving a semi-salute from the man in return.

Shaw struggled to affix his old army rucksack to the pannier rack on his bicycle, and decided to carry it on his back instead. After all, he thought, it was only a mile or so to the cathedral. Then a voice with a note of irrepressible mirth rang out.

'My dear Padre, you haven't changed a bit!'

Shaw looked up from the various straps and buckles on the rucksack to the man standing in front of him. He was slightly built and boyish looking, with a fringe of hair which flopped down over the right hand side of his head from beneath his hat brim. Shaw wondered if some mistake had been made.

'Palgrave?' he asked tentatively. 'Tom Palgrave?'

'The very same, Padre,' said the man, extending his hand. 'Look here, I can hardly keep calling you Padre. Will Shaw do?'

Shaw nodded and shook Palgrave's hand warmly as the latter continued to talk.

'Even if you had changed, which you haven't, I'd have recognised you from that old thing.' He pointed to Shaw's rucksack. 'Look, you can still see your name and service number on it,' he said. 'Just about, anyway.'

'Oh yes,' said Shaw, looking at the faded inscription on the bag which he dimly remembered painting there when he started out as a military chaplain.

'I fear you flatter me, Palgrave,' he continued. 'I suspect I have faded almost as much as that lettering.'

'Nonsense old boy,' said Palgrave. 'The hair's gone a bit grey I'll admit but you're just as tall and slim as ever you were and you still look a bit like that chap from the papers, what's his name, the one they call the Gloomy Dean.'

'William Inge,' said Shaw. 'I hope *not*. He must be in his

seventies by now. You, however, do not look a day older than when we last met.'

Palgrave chuckled. 'Well that's good to know as forty hoves into view. I put it down to ascetic living and remaining unmarried. The life of a cathedral organist doesn't afford much opportunity for debauchery.'

'I am glad to hear it,' said Shaw. 'When did we last meet?' he asked.

'It was at that rather dreary place in Aldershot just before demob,' answered Palgrave. '1919 – January, I think. Some silly camp-concert that nobody cared much for as we were all desperate to get home the next day.'

'Ah yes,' said Shaw, and stood back as the train began to pull out of the station with a hissing of steam and a shrill blast on its whistle. He looked at Palgrave, who looked little different to the young subaltern with whom he had shared a bunker when on the front lines as a military chaplain.

He realised he had no recollection of a camp-concert in Aldershot. His chief memory of Palgrave was that he was the man who had broken the news of the Armistice to him on the eleventh of November 1918, shaking him awake in the middle of the night, shortly after a frantic motor-bicycle messenger had arrived.

'It's over, Padre,' he had said excitedly. 'Jerry's declared.'

Shaw, still half asleep, had been confused by the sporting metaphor.

'Declared?' he asked. 'But the Germans don't play cricket.'

'Oh do wake *up*, Padre,' insisted Palgrave. 'I mean they've chucked it in. All hostilities to cease at eleven hundred hours.'

'Is it a dream?' Shaw had asked, rubbing his eyes. 'Or

some sort of mistake?'

'It's true sir, nor a word of a lie,' said the orderly who had just come in to the dugout, corporal something or other; Shaw could no longer remember his name.

'Signal just come through from Brigade not five minutes ago,' continued the loquacious little man as he pottered around, fussing over various items of kit. 'Took it meself from the despatcher. He's riding all along the line, what with the telephones being out after that land-mine. The colonel wants all officers on parade at oh-five-hundred and he asked for you and the RC padre as well, and the Methodist chap. Wants a bit of thanks offered up, I shouldn't wonder. Shall you want your surplice, or just your number twos, sir?'

Shaw had risen from his bunk and knelt beside it immediately, reciting the General Thanksgiving from the little prayer book he always kept by his side. Palgrave, who was a religious man, knelt also; the corporal and a couple of other NCOs waiting for orders by the dugout entrance took their helmets off and stared at the ground with a certain degree of embarrassment.

That had been Shaw's abiding memory of Palgrave and it had come as a pleasant surprise that the man was now living only a few miles away.

'You need not have met me at the station,' said Shaw.

'Rot,' said Palgrave. 'I haven't seen you for fifteen years and besides, the under-organist is playing at Evensong tonight. We've a lot to catch up on. You can tell me all your news as we walk. Let me take your bag.'

Palgrave shrugged Shaw's rucksack onto his shoulders and they walked out of the station onto Gabriel Hill, the long road which gently led upwards to the centre of Midchester.

'This bun-fight you're here for,' said Palgrave. 'Remind

me what it's all about. I saw your name on the attendees notice in the cloisters, which is why I dropped you a line.'

'The Parish Eucharist Society is holding a conference,' said Shaw. 'I, as a local minister with some affinity for their cause, have been asked to give some talks. '

'Are they the lot that want HC – Holy Communion, I mean, held more often?' asked Palgrave.

'Correct.'

'And you thought it would be a good opportunity to escape the lady wife for a bit of a spree, eh?'

Had Shaw not had an old acquaintance with Palgrave, he might have taken offence, but he remembered the man well enough to know there was no ill intent in the remark.

'I would hardly call a few days in the company of some dusty and probably very High Church clergymen a "spree",' said Shaw with a wry smile. 'No, the organisers have a generous benefactor who is paying me handsomely.'

'Ah, you *are* going on the spree, you old devil!' said Palgrave gleefully.

'Allow me to finish,' chided Shaw good-naturedly. 'The payment will be donated entirely to our church fabric fund, which is sorely depleted.'

'Just think yourself lucky you've got a bed in my billet,' said Palgrave. 'The other delegates are putting up at Diocesan House, which as far as I know has no indoor plumbing and hasn't had a lick of paint since the days of Queen Anne.'

'It is indeed most kind of you,' said Shaw. 'I could, of course, have taken the train to and from Midchester every day but the railway fares would have been considerable. There is also the matter of the last train to Addenham leaving at 9 pm, whereas the conference dinners, which I ought to attend, will continue later than that, I fear.'

'Dinners?' laughed Palgrave. 'I knew it. It's just an excuse to relive your undergraduate days. I'd better be careful you and the other old fossils don't try to dunk me in the Midwell when you're all sozzled on port!'

Shaw laughed and the conversation continued in that manner for the rest of the journey. They talked of the past in that way that men do who have who have not seen each other for many years. There was no awkwardness and they picked up their friendship as if they had last met only a few days ago.

By the time they arrived at the cathedral, they had given each other potted summaries of the intervening years; Shaw had talked of his family and his work as a parish priest in Lower Addenham, and Palgrave of his failed attempt to make his fortune in the former German East Africa colony after it was taken over by the British.

'I didn't make a penny out there,' he said glumly. 'Trouble is I don't know the first thing about jute, and I was supposed to be farming the stuff. All I've ever been good at is playing the organ, and there weren't many opportunities for *that* up-country in British East.

'So back I came, and managed to bag a job doing what I love. I had absolutely no idea you were living so close to the ancestral home. I only came back a few months ago though, once I took up the post of organist here at the cathedral.'

'Ah yes,' said Shaw. 'You were at, where was it, Wells before?'

'Truro,' said Palgrave. About as remote as one can get. Jobs were scarce after the war and I had to take what I could get, and well, it wasn't the sort of place friends could drop by to for a Friday-to-Sunday. So when I saw the job going at Midchester in the *Church Times* I leaped at the chance.'

'And now you are back,' replied Shaw. 'Your family seat is still the house over the river from here? Now what was it called, Mere Lodge?' asked Shaw.

'Mead Lodge,' corrected Palgrave with a chuckle, 'but your first guess was more accurate. It's a mere lodge all right. Nearly all the land's gone now, and the money with it. My sister, Millie – Mrs Reynolds, I mean – looks after it. Ought to be me of course – son and heir and all that – but I've never had much aptitude for that sort of thing.'

'Your sister has a husband, I assume?' asked Shaw.

'Had,' replied Palgrave. 'Bought it at Arras, I'm sorry to say. I probably didn't mention it to you back then. Well, one didn't, did one? Unless it was someone very close. There were so many.'

'Yes indeed,' said Shaw. There was silence for a moment, until Shaw broke it. 'This is a splendid street, I must say,' he exclaimed, as they walked into the Cathedral Close. Shaw was familiar with the cathedral itself, having attended numerous services there as part of his diocesan obligations, but he was less familiar with the surrounding buildings, particularly the Close, the little lane that contained the houses of most of the clergy.

'Superb, isn't it?' said Palgrave. 'That's the Deanery there,' he said, pointing to a large double-fronted Restoration house, 'and that's the Chancellor's place next door. They get less grand as we go along. This is my place.'

They paused in front of a little brick-built terraced cottage with ivy climbing the walls. Palgrave opened the door and they walked into a well-appointed sitting room, larger than one might expect, with a piano in one corner and a pair of French doors that led out to a small garden beyond.

'Comes as part of the job,' said Palgrave. 'Of course, I could live at the Lodge but although it's not far as the crow flies, it's quite a long bicycle ride because one has to cross the river at Flintham Ford a mile up the road. You're up here in the bedroom. Come on, I'll show you.'

The younger man bounded up a steep flight of stairs to a small bedroom with a sloping ceiling, sparsely furnished with a single iron bedstead and a dresser, and a text on the wall, as thought it were a servant's bedroom. Through the little casement window, in the last of the daylight, Shaw could make out the River Midwell beyond the garden wall, and the twinkling lights that were just coming on in a distant house beyond the meadow.

'Hullo,' said Palgrave, peering out of the window. 'Sis is wasting electricity again I see. That's the Lodge over there. She ought to be going around with a candle stub, the way she goes on about our impending financial doom.'

'I feel rather ill at ease turning you out of your bedroom like this,' said Shaw.

'Nonsense,' said Palgrave cheerfully. 'I'll sleep anywhere. The sofa downstairs will be perfectly comfortable. There ought to be another bedroom but that was turned into the ablutions years ago. Still, a few centuries ago it would have been a monastic cell for the likes of us and a wash in the river, so one mustn't complain. Oh, I know I'm not ordained, but I might as well be. Vow of chastity and poverty, and all that. Comes with the job.'

'Chastity?' said Shaw with a raised eyebrow. 'You have never desired to marry?'

Palgrave laughed. 'There's not much difficulty keeping chaste when you're penniless! What woman in her right mind would have someone like me, poor as a church mouse and with an ancestral home falling around his ears? And a dowager sister living there as well. No, I've had a few narrow scrapes but I'm set for a life-long bachelor.'

'You are still young – relatively,' chided Shaw. 'One never knows.'

'The pleasures of the flesh are much over-rated, if you ask me,' said Palgrave with a smile. 'One thing I do rather miss though is a woman's touch about the place. Cooking, and mending socks and so on.'

'You have no servants?'

'We have *a* servant. In the singular. Poor old Mrs Snelgrove. And she's only a daily and eighty if she's a day. We other ranks – the minor canons and so on – have to share her. She said she'd leave a cold supper for us but knowing her, that will mean an unopened tin of luncheon meat.'

Shaw laughed. 'Servants are hard to come by these days. We at the vicarage are very lucky to have Hettie, but I fear in a few years time it will be impossible to retain her.'

'We won't have any in a few *weeks* if things carry on the way they are,' replied Palgrave grimly.

'Ah,' replied Shaw. 'Am I to take it you are referring to your new Dean?'

'Yes,' sighed Palgrave. 'He only seems to have been here since yesterday, and already he's trying to turn the place into some sort of utopia. You know all about him of course?'

'Only what the newspapers say. I met him briefly at a diocesan meeting and attended his inauguration, but cannot claim to know him.'

'The papers are mostly right,' said Palgrave. 'But look here, I can't face talking about *him* on an empty stomach. Let's have supper. There's a bottle of half-decent hock somewhere.'

Shaw was momentarily distracted by a movement in the corner of his eye. A flash of something light-coloured in beyond the window. Was it someone in the garden? He

19

looked again, but the little yard was empty.

'Is there a path beyond the garden?' he asked.

'Yes,' replied Palgrave. 'There's a right of way that runs between the garden wall and the river. Why?'

'No reason,' murmured Shaw. He suddenly felt tired and realised he was rather hungry.

'May I put my things away?' he asked. 'I am assuming your Mrs Snelgrove will not be unpacking my rucksack.'

Palgrave chuckled. 'She'd most likely throw it in the river if you asked such a thing,' he said. 'You can have the top drawer here,' he said, pointing to the plain wooden dresser in the corner. 'I've cleared it out for you.'

He pulled the drawer open to indicate it, and then shut it. 'Oh, while I'm here, have a look at this.'

He opened the drawer below and took out a faded photograph. 'This is my memento drawer. I keep all the useless sentimental old things in here, and speaking of which, here's a picture of two of them. It's the only one we're both in, I think.'

He handed a photograph of uniformed men in rows to Shaw; he scanned the serried ranks of officers, non-commissioned officers and private soldiers, stiffly erect in their dress uniforms on some sunny parade ground, in what now seemed another world.

'"B Company, Haig Barracks, Saint-Quentin, June 1917". Well, well,' said Shaw. 'I have the same photograph somewhere. I believe that is me there, next to, now what was his name? Simpson? The Methodist chaplain.'

'Simpkins,' corrected Palgrave. '"Simpering Simpkins", we used to call him, do you remember? That's me on the far left with the other subalterns. I'd only just arrived from staff college and hadn't had my new six-shooter issued. Look, you can see my holster's empty and the lanyard's just dangling off my Sam Browne. How did the RSM not notice that? Lord, what an absolute shower!'

Shaw smiled, and then felt a prick of emotion as he realised how many of the men in that picture had not come back. Palgrave must have sensed it too, as he took the photograph and replaced it in the drawer.

'Ah well,' he said wistfully. 'All in the past now. Let's have a bit of supper, eh?'

Shaw nodded, but just before Palgrave briskly closed the drawer, he noticed at the back, amongst a pile of old photographs and documents, a canvas holster. But this one was not empty, and the last of the daylight from the window glinted suddenly on the black handgrip of a Webley revolver.

Chapter Two

S ome time later, a short distance away in the Deanery, a less convivial conversation was taking place. Evensong had finished and the Dean's duties for the day had ended. He and his wife were seated at opposite ends of a rather large and ornate Victorian dining table in a rather large and ornate dining room.

'I don't see why *I* should be expected to cook,' said Mrs Vale, a timid, mousy woman whose frustrated desire to assert herself appeared mainly in the form of henpecking her husband, or sulking, with the pretence of a headache to mask her bad moods.

She picked half-heartedly at the undernourished pork chop that the servant had recently placed in front of her before departing without waiting to be told to do so.

'You know I wasn't brought up to that sort of thing,' she said peevishly. 'No woman in my family was. My maternal grandfather was...'

'Was Suffragen Bishop of Ely,' said Vale, smiling as sincerely as he was able. 'So you have told me often, Elizabeth. But as *I* have told *you* often in reply, times have changed since our young day. The Chapter – the cathedral staff and so on – ought no longer to have domestic servants. It is not fitting for the modern age, and besides, we cannot afford it.'

'Very well,' said Mrs Vale. 'I expect I shall have to enrol

in some sort of cookery class, with housewives from the town and gas rings, and sixpences in meters. A fine Christian example that would be, I'm sure.'

Vale's smile remained fixed on his face. The daily tragedy of their unhappy marriage had worsened over the years. Perhaps if they had had children, it might have been different; but there was no use pondering that.

He had once found her attractive for her progressive views, but as she aged, he realised that she had not advanced intellectually as he had done, and was still mentally living in the world of 1914.

For her, liberalism and the Bloomsbury Group were still the highest form of radical politics; whilst he had breathed deeply of the wind of real political change which had swept across the world in recent years. He was determined that every British institution should be made to set its sails to that wind, the Church of England included, and nobody, not even his wife, should stand in his way.

He thought grimly of a recent theory posited by a Biblical scholar – that Jesus had married – to be preposterous. Crucifixion was one thing, but for the Son of God to voluntarily give himself up to a lifetime of domestic strife was beyond all rational belief.

'You shall not need to cook anything,' he exclaimed brightly, doing his best to sound encouraging.

'I suppose you'll make shift with sandwiches, is that it?' replied Mrs Vale.

'Kindly allow me to finish,' said her husband. 'You shall not need to cook because one of the changes I intend to make is to re-open the refectory.'

'Is this another of your reforms?'

'Hardly, my dear. It is in fact a return to a more monastic way of life, so the reactionaries – or the conservatives, as they prefer to call themselves – in the Chapter ought to be happy about it.'

'I have no idea what you are talking about.'

'I shall explain,' said Vale condescendingly. 'Instead of the members of the Chapter having domestic servants to keep house and cook for them individually, I am going to bring back the medieval practice of communal meals in the refectory. It is rarely used, which is a waste of resources.'

'You mean…we shall have to eat in some sort of…canteen? Like factory workers?'

'In principle yes. We shall be showing solidarity with the workers, in our own way. It will also save money.'

Mrs Vale looked troubled. 'If it's all the same with you, I *shall* make do with sandwiches. Or a boiled egg. I'm sure I can manage that. I have no desire to live as if it's the middle ages, or some sort of workers' soviet.'

'You must do as you think best, my dear,' said Vale, in a tone which indicated that the subject was closed.

'I thought you said money didn't matter,' said his wife slyly. 'That those who thought about it too much, like the Chancellor and the Treasurer, were worldly and capitalistic.'

'Indeed I did, and indeed they are,' replied Vale. 'But that will be to my advantage at the Chapter meeting tomorrow. It will be difficult for my opponents to claim that the re-institution of communal dining, which I believe fell into abeyance after the Reformation, is something new and strange, and it will be impossible for them to claim it will cost too much money, when it will in fact save a considerable amount. "Check mate", I think.'

He chuckled to himself as he chewed on his pork chop which had by now gone cold.

Len 'Skinny' Skinner trudged wearily along a back street near Midchester's river docks. It had been a long day and he'd been working hard. He wondered about dropping in to the Red Lion on the way home, but decided against it since he was on his own. You never knew who might be about.

Skinner lived up to his nickname; he was slightly built (he preferred to think of himself as wiry) with a rodent-like face, made more rat-like by a whiskery thin moustache. He had heavily oiled hair with a permanent wave in it, after the fashion set by a well known 'crooner', and he had once pushed a man through a plate glass window for saying it made him look like a 'nancy boy'.

It wasn't, he thought, that he *enjoyed* violence, it was just something he did when it was needed and didn't think about, like most people wouldn't think twice about swatting a fly. A prison doctor had once asked him all sorts of blasted silly questions, and told him there was a name for people like him that didn't feel things like other people did, but he'd forgotten what it was; and anyway, he didn't care. Other people could go hang.

A well-cut but gaudy suit and tie completed his look, but with a cap rather than a hat. It didn't do to appear *too* flash round here, he thought. This wasn't London, and didn't he know it.

Skinner had his finger in all sort of pies in Midchester, mainly those connected with the racing fraternity and various financial instruments thereto. In short, he was a bookmaker. It being illegal to place bets outside race courses, he made a good living taking wagers from people in the town then placing them at the course, either in person or via the telephone, for a fee. He was good at it, having a head for figures.

He had started young in the east end of London but had soon found that his business skills attracted attention from the wrong sort of people, and he had learned to defend himself. Not with his fists if he could avoid it, but with a cut-throat razor he always carried.

You didn't need to be a big bloke, he had realised, to intimidate people. You just needed to look as if you were prepared to hurt the other chap more than he was prepared to hurt you.

A razor was a fine weapon because it was legal to carry – even if a copper searched you, you just told him you were taking it to be sharpened and there was nothing he could do about it. A knife was only for foreign types like the Maltese mob, and a gun was for lunatics; that would likely mean a death sentence if you used it. A cosh was all right if you had the element of surprise, but couldn't really be used to threaten anybody.

A razor, now, that was different. Just taking it out and showing it, closed, was usually enough to get difficult people to comply, and then flicked open if you needed a greater threat. And if you actually had to use it, well, just a swift nick to the earlobe was enough to draw a lot of blood and terrify even hardened criminals.

Eventually, even his skills of intimidation were not enough. Too many foreign gangs were moving into London; the yiddishers were running the East End, Italians were taking over Soho, and Camden was full of Maltese. It was getting, he reflected, so that a decent Englishman could no longer earn a living in his own home town.

On a day out to Midchester racecourse, Skinner had got talking to some local men in a pub and he had realised the place was ripe for the taking. They were yokels out here, hayseeds, no business sense. So he had upped sticks and moved here and before long had begun building his little empire with a combination of hard work and threatening behaviour.

It hadn't taken long for him to have the betting business sewn up, plus the loan-sharking that went with it, and he had even got a bit of a protection racket going and one or two girls working for him. But now, he was beginning to think big. Really big.

He arrived back at the little terraced house he called home, in a seedy back street. He let himself in with his latch key and hung his raincoat and cap up on the hall-stand, set against a backdrop of peeling Victorian wallpaper.

A blowsy looking blonde woman appeared from the downstairs parlour. The sound of a sentimental song from a gramophone drifted out into the corridor. She had clearly been drinking, but by the dim light of the gasolier she looked, to Skinner, dangerously enticing.

'Hello dear,' said the woman. 'You look done in. Aw. Why not come and have a little rum-and-pep with me. I'll make you feel better.'

'Leave off Queenie,' said Skinner, though he felt a tingle of excitement pass through his body as he looked at the woman's curvaceous form straining beneath a dress made of some tight sheer material. He swallowed. 'I told you I keep things strictly businesslike with my employees.'

Never sample your own supply, thought Skinner. He'd heard that from a dope peddler up Limehouse way. Once you started on that, you were done for. You were 'hooked', as the saying went. He untied his tie and hung it up on the hall-stand, then unfixed his collar.

'Aw, that's what I like about you, Skinny,' said the

27

woman. 'A proper gent.'

'Told you not to call me that.'

The woman giggled. 'What, a proper gent?'

'You know what I mean. It's Mr Skinner to you.'

Queenie pouted.

'Oh all right, suit yourself, *Mr Skinner*. While we're on the subject, why don't you use *my* name instead of that silly one you've given me?'

'Mavis sounds cheap,' replied Skinner. 'Queenie suits you better. More…classy. Now let me be, I'm tired.'

'Oh all right then, suit yourself,' said the woman. 'I'll get back to my convent before it closes, shall I?'

'You ain't a nun.'

'No, but I feel like one. You don't even send me any gentlemen callers no more. Didn't think I'd miss *that*, but any port in a storm, as they say. What's a girl supposed to do all day?'

'You just put your feet up and relax,' said Skinner, as he began to climb the stairs. 'Told you I'll pay you for not working. Save your energy. I've got plans for you.'

Queenie looked at him with a confused expression on her face, then shrugged and went back into her room.

Shaw awoke later than he had hoped; he had forgotten to wind his little travel alarm clock and it had run down in the night. He sat up quickly, almost bumping his head on the low eaves of the cottage bedroom. He checked his watch and realised he would have to hurry if he was to make the opening session of the conference. It would look bad, he reflected, if he were to arrive late on the first morning.

He and Palgrave had stayed up far later than they ought to have done, talking and reminiscing over one – or was it two – bottles of claret and some port as well. He rubbed his eyes. The bachelor life of a cathedral organist was obviously far more worldly than that of a married parish priest, and he was not used to such late nights.

He prayed by his bedside and then made use of the little bathroom next door, which was mercifully more modern than the rest of the little house, with hot and cold laid on and a good supply of towels. He hummed a hymn tune to himself as he shaved at the basin. Although the sash window was of frosted glass, on this mild September morning it was partially raised, and he could see through to the little garden below, and the path and river beyond.

A man was walking swiftly along the path, dressed in a dark coat and bowler hat; he had a spaniel on a lead which he was attempting to control by tugging, but the dog was having none of it and ran round his master's legs, looping the lead around them as he went. The man said something indistinct, released himself and hurried along.

Shaw smiled, and then frowned; the figure he had almost caught sight of yesterday evening in the same place could not have been walking or even dawdling on the path; he had been standing stock still and had then suddenly moved. Had he been watching the house, and departed when he had seen Shaw at the window?

Shaw splashed cold water on his face and rinsed off the last of the shaving soap. He was getting carried away again with plots and intrigues. There had been no such excitements in his life for over a year now, he reflected, and it was vain and self-indulgent to think there ever might be again.

He put on his dark lounge suit; tweeds were too informal for a conference, but a cassock would perhaps be overdoing it; and besides, he had not brought one. He heard the sound of movement in the room below, and checked his watch; Palgrave had said he would be leaving early to take a choir practice at the Cathedral School, so who was downstairs?

Cautiously he descended the little winding staircase and was slightly relieved to see a bulky lady in an apron, with grey hair in a bun, pottering around the little dining table which also served as Palgrave's desk.

'Why he can't keep things tidy I'll never understand,' she muttered to herself, then looked up.

'Oh, you're up then,' said the woman abruptly.

'Yes,' replied Shaw. 'A little later than I had hoped. You are Mrs Snelgrove, I take it?'

'That's right,' replied the woman, wiping her hands on her apron. 'And you'll be Mr Shaw I suppose.'

'That is correct.'

'Expect his nibs has told you all sorts of tales about me.'

'His…nibs?'

'Mr Palgrave.'

'Ah. No, he merely led me to understand that his servant was a much older woman.'

Shaw noticed Mrs Snelgrove blush slightly and was pleased to have broken the ice; he was familiar with the type of elderly domestic servant who affects to dislike her employer.

'Flattery'll get you nowhere, as they say,' said Mrs Snelgrove with a slight smile. 'I'm seventy and that's old by anyone's standards. 'Here, have your breakfast afore it gets cold. Not much, eggs and bacon, but it will keep you going until lunch time if you're to give speeches, as Mr Palgrave says you are to.'

'That is correct, and thank you, Mrs Snelgrove.'

'Mrs S is good enough for me. I've no airs.'

'Very good then, Mrs S it is,' said Shaw as he tucked in to the breakfast. 'May I trouble you for a cup of tea?'

Shaw wondered if he had pushed his luck as the woman disappeared into the little kitchen off the living room. When she reappeared she had a teapot, cup and saucer in her hands, and she placed them on the table next to him .

'Course you can, sir,' she said. 'No trouble. But I can't stop to be mother, as I've the other gentlemen to see to. I've got two of the minor canons' beds to make this morning.'

'A lot of work for you, Mrs S,' said Shaw as he poured himself a cup of tea.

'*I* don't mind it,' said Mrs Snelgrove as she straightened the haphazardly arranged piles of sheet music on the table. 'Some of the young clergymen as works in the cathedral need straightening out, as you might say. Need a mother. Or grandmother, I suppose, these days,' she added with a chuckle.

'And you picks up all sorts of bits of useful information in such a job,' she continued. 'Now my husband – that's Mr Snelgrove, of the Sudbury Snelgroves – he was Steward of the Close afore he retired with his chest. Did odd jobs and kept the place in good order, as it were. He's been bored to tears since he retired, but I tells him all the news. That egg all right for you dear, I mean, sir?'

'Excellent, thank you,'

'Mind you,' sniffed Mrs Snelgrove, who appeared to have forgotten that she had other gentlemen to attend to, 'mind you, I don't suppose I shall be needed much longer, the way things are going round here. You'll have heard the rumours?'

Shaw was tempted to say 'one ought never to listen to rumours' but decided it would sound priggish. He had discerned from Palgrave the night before that all was not quite well with the new Dean, but had not wished to pry.

'It's the new Dean,' said Mrs Snelgrove, folding her arms. 'Now I'm not one to talk behind people's backs, it ain't Christian, but he gives me the pip, as they say. And not just me, the other servants too.'

'And why is that?' asked Shaw cautiously.

'Why? I'll tell you for why. Because he wants *rid* of us, that's why. Yus. Says we cost too much. Cost too much! I should like to see a gentleman such as that live on what we're paid! I only keep going because I gets the old age pension on top.'

'We must hope that *is* only a rumour, Mrs S,' said Shaw, as he finished his breakfast. 'Now I ought to be going. Could you direct me to the Diocesan House, please?'

'It's off the Green sir, you'll see it from the Cloisters,' said Mrs Snelgrove as she walked to the door and opened it. 'You have a nice time at your conference,' she added. 'Which is more than I'll have today, I daresay. The Chapter's meeting this forenoon, and that's when they'll be deciding to get rid of us.'

'Courage, Mrs S. We must be optimistic,' said Shaw.

'Eh?' asked the servant.

'We must look on the bright side.'

'If you say so, sir,' said Mrs Snelgrove glumly, and then trudged off down the Close towards the house of the minor canons.

Doctor Adams, the Chancellor, was seething with anger as he prepared himself for Matins in the cathedral vestry. He snapped at two of the choirboys for chattering, and immediately regretted it. He took a deep breath and prayed inwardly for calm. After a few moments he felt more composed, and peeped through the large double doors into the cathedral.

Weekday Matins was normally a sparsely attended service. It was more an assembly for the choir school really, although it was sometimes attended by a few early tourists and local people. Today, however, a steady stream of men was entering the nave from the cloisters; they were the delegates from the Parish Communion Conference who were meeting at Diocesan House and attending services as part of their programme.

The sight lifted his mood slightly. The conference had been his idea; well, not entirely his, if truth be told; it had been suggested to him by an acquaintance in the world of business. 'Why not hold a conference?' the man had asked. 'They are all the rage these days. People pay handsomely.'

The conference was part of his fund-raising programme which he had begun under the old Dean; but that venerable and agreeable cleric had then retired suddenly due to ill health. His replacement had somewhat different views on the role of finance in the church. Adams felt his anger rise again and he remembered the letter he had received that morning.

Adams had spoken to Reverend Vale, the Dean, a week ago about the conference, but the man had replied with less than half an hour's notice! And he had not even had the decency to do it in person, but via a grubby letter, in an unsealed envelope so that, presumably, the servants could read it before delivery. It was underhand, and, thought Adams, quite deliberate.

He rummaged beneath his surplice and felt in his cassock pocket for the missive, which he looked at once more.

My Dear Chancellor,

I thank you for your invitation to address the delegates of the Parish Communion Conference on the 19th inst. As you know, I do not think the cathedral should be involved in events for commercial gain, but as this was arranged under my predecessor, I am willing to allow it to take place as an exception. I do not, however, wish to endorse it by some form of official address and I trust you will be more than capable of doing so in my place.

It occurs to me that not only is this conference distasteful as it is intended for financial gain, but because of its subject matter. The church, I believe, should not concern itself with pettifogging discussions about the frequency of entirely symbolic rituals such as Holy Communion. Rather, it should concentrate on feeding the poor with the bread of Earth, before it attempts to do so with that of Heaven.

The letter ended with *per procurationem* initials from the cathedral secretary. The man had not even bothered to sign it himself. Adams screwed the letter up into a ball and thrust it into his pocket.

'"The bread of Earth" indeed,' he muttered in disgust.

'Sir?' enquired the crucifer, a sixth-former from the choir school, who had already lifted up his gilded cross and was making his way to the vestry doors with a gaggle of choirboys behind him.

'Nothing boy, nothing,' said Adams. 'Let us begin.'

As the procession emerged from the vestry the organ music increased in volume, and the ranks of black-clad visiting clergy rustled to their feet from their chairs. Adams realised he would have to improvise an address and began thinking about what he would say. As the procession halted in front of the high altar, Adams and the crucifer bowed, followed by the choirboys, and then began to take their places in the stalls.

Adams looked up to his left briefly as he passed through the rood screen, and noticed that Vale was sitting up in the King's Gallery, alone and imperious, gazing down on the proceedings below like some Roman emperor at the Coliseum.

He felt that uncontrollable surge of anger again; the man was not even bothering to pretend he had a prior engagement that prevented him from addressing the conference. He was sitting up there, thought Adams, as if he was God Almighty Himself.

As he took his place in the choir stalls, he could not help thinking of a line from the Magnificat:

He hath put down the mighty from their seats…

Mrs Vale, who did not attend cathedral services except on Sundays, was in a quandary. The post had arrived slightly later than usual, and her husband had not been able, as was his habit, to intercept the letters the moment the servant brought them in to the breakfast table.

She had dawdled over her morning tea until Vale had left for Matins, and then considered the letters on the salver in front of her. There were three; one was a circular from one of the charities to which she subscribed (charity work was her principal occupation); the other was from an elderly cousin given to writing thinly-disguised begging letters. She decided to read both later. The third, however, was the one that had put her in a quandary.

It was addressed to her husband, in a feminine hand. She had seen that handwriting on letters before, once or twice; and her husband had swiftly put those into his pocket each time, murmuring something about perusing them in his study. She had a fairly good idea who it was from.

She picked up the letter, and looked with slight distaste at the flowing writing and expensive stationery; it was in stark contrast to her own precise, small lettering and the plain paper and envelopes that her husband allowed her from Woolworth's, it being one of his foibles to imitate what he thought were the habits of the 'common man' in non-essential matters.

After checking that the servant was nowhere nearby, she took a deep breath and grabbed the letter, opening it quickly with her little finger. She could, she thought, have steamed it open; that was what happened in books; but the servant was sure to see if she did such a thing with the kettle in the kitchen. Vale had not seen the letter delivered, and thus, need never know it had gone missing.

Her worst fears were confirmed when she read the brief note inside.

My darling
I must speak with you. I shan't let you leave me, whatever the reason. I will meet you in the usual place. Nobody need know.
All my love,
M.

Mrs Vale felt tears prick her eyes, and blinked them back. I *must* be sensible, she thought. I must think *rationally*.

Of course, it was no real surprise. It had happened before; in fact it was one of the reasons that her husband's family had pulled strings and got him a new job in another part of the country; to avoid damaging the church with a public scandal involving a clergyman who was already getting a reputation for being rather too unconventional. Their marriage was outwardly unscathed, and her husband had even had a promotion into the bargain; from Sub-Dean of Aldminster to Dean of Midchester.

She knew her husband was attractive to other women; she knew that there was something about clergymen, particularly good looking ones, that attracted a Certain Sort of Woman. There had been others before this one, of course.

The last one had made a show of piety; oh yes, she thought, they were always outwardly pious because they thought a clergyman would expect it of them, but it was clear now that woman's attendance at services had been for reasons other than religious ones. Everyone had known, of course, and what was worse, she was the last to find out The entire Chapter at Aldminster had known before she did.

The humiliation! Why should she be made to suffer for her husband's sin? She had, of course, her own sins to atone for – although, she thought to herself, was what she indulged in really a sin? It certainly was not mentioned in the Ten Commandments. No, hers was a mere…pecadillo.

Well, thought Mrs Vale, as she screwed the letter up into a ball and clenched her fists, I will *not* be humiliated again.

Shaw arrived a little late at Diocesan House and was still completing his registration form for the conference as the other delegates began filing through the cloisters into the cathedral for Matins. The service, along with Evensong, formed part of the conference programme and all delegates were encouraged to attend.

Shaw hurriedly finished off his form and followed the last of the stragglers into the cathedral. The crowd were much as he had expected – mostly middle-aged clerics of the High Church party; one or two he recognised dimly but there was nobody he knew well enough to talk to, and besides, the service was clearly about to begin as the procession of clergy and choir had already started.

He noticed that nearly all the chairs in the eastern portion of the nave were taken; to sit any further back would make it difficult to hear. He wondered whether to push his way through the rows of seating to one of the few free places, but decided it would be overly disruptive. Fortunately, just before the service began, an elderly verger realised he had nowhere to sit, and with a discreet 'this way, sir,' showed him to a small double pew – a bench really – at right angles to the nave on the corner of the south transept.

'This is reserved for vergers,' said the man amiably, 'but I think we may make an exception. Unfortunately you will have to crane your neck slightly to see the altar.'

Shaw thanked the man and moved to the pew just as the choir began the introit, the opening sentences of the service set to music. It was to a setting, he seemed to recall, by Orlando Gibbons, that great seventeenth century church composer.

> Rend your heart, and not your garments, and turn unto
> the Lord…

Shaw felt the slow cadences of the motet sweep over him and looked upwards, seeing the pillars soaring up to the vaulted roof; the September sun shone through the Victorian stained glass of the east window, casting colourful light on the polished stone floor of the nave. He was not used to cathedral services; his own parish church did its best with a small choir made up mostly of farmhands and schoolboys, but it was as nothing compared to this.

Quickly, however, the introit was over and the presiding cleric – the Chancellor – began to recite the long opening exhortation. Shaw, who knew the service by heart, felt his mind wander. His eyes were drawn upwards to the large, decrepit looking wooden gallery which spanned the north transept directly opposite him.

That, he realised, was where the controversial Dean Vale had placed the Red Flag, the Irish tricolour and another flag that Shaw did not fully recognise – Indian, perhaps? He had not been in the cathedral to see them before but had read of the controversy in the *Church Times*. It seemed a somewhat childish and overly political gesture; why deliberately antagonise others with secular symbols?

Then Shaw noticed that above the flags, a man was seated. He recognised him as Vale, looking down on the nave with his fingers steepled in front of him. Curious, thought Shaw. Why was the man up there and not in the choir stalls? He took out the conference programme from his pocket and discretely consulted it: yes, there it was, for the first day, Choral Matins, with address by the Dean.

Shaw then was obliged to kneel as the exhortation ended and the opening prayers began. He thought no more of Vale until the address. He sensed something of an uncomfortable atmosphere as the red-faced Chancellor, breathing heavily, welcomed the delegates on behalf of the Dean, who, he explained, was unfortunately not giving a welcome speech as advertised but who was, however, no doubt watching the proceedings with interest from 'on high' in the King's Gallery with the 'regalia that has caused a certain amount of interest from the press'.

There was a polite murmur signifying something between amusement and puzzlement. He heard the verger next to him mutter something which sounded less than charitable. A few heads turned upwards to look at the gallery, but when Shaw did likewise, Vale seemed to be looking away.

Chapter Three

How, thought Adams, had it come to this? He looked up at the vaulted ceiling and huge clear leaded windows of the cathedral's Chapter House, the institution's common room, in which all important decisions were made. Its walls, arranged in a pentagon, were lined with statues and portraits of previous Bishops, Deans, Chancellors and other worthies, the stern, time-darkened faces of the past looking down on him and seeming, as he thought, to find him wanting.

He sometimes found himself thinking such thoughts while he waited for the weekly Chapter Meeting to begin. He was a stickler for order and punctuality, and always arrived first with piles of papers and notes for the meeting, which he would go through to ensure he knew what he needed to say.

How had it come to this? How had the simple message of a first century Jewish carpenter, that the Word was made flesh and dwelt among us, that man could be not merely a helpless observer of, but an active *partaker* in, the Divine Nature – how had it been so distorted? How had it become so encumbered, weighed down with so much dogma and worldly concern?

He looked at the piles of papers in front of him; to keep merely one cathedral functioning required organisational and financial acumen on a scale that would have daunted even the most rapacious captains of industry.

He sighed, and nodded a greeting as the first members of the Chapter began to file into the room for the meeting. They were well-meaning fellows; but weak-willed or elderly, for the most part, or, as in the case of Palgrave the organist and Jones, the Precentor, seemingly unwilling to do anything that might risk the safety of their positions.

He thought again briefly of a recurring idea of entering some sort of monastic institution, of shuffling off all his mortal concerns and dedicating himself afresh to a life of prayer and simple labour. But it was hopeless, he thought. No, he corrected himself. Not hopeless; it was simply wrong. If men of principle abandoned the church, then only the men of *no* principle would remain.

And that was the rub. The cathedral was unique among its kind, having what was known as Royal Entailment, a complex legal standing which meant the place was not run like most others. The Bishop was largely absent (and at the present moment had begun wintering in the south of France, despite it only being September). Dean Vale had almost complete control, and could simply over-ride the concerns of the Chapter in all but the most minor matters.

That had not been a problem for Adams when he had served under the old Dean, a true Christian gentleman now sadly deceased, with whom he had seen eye to eye on all important matters. But the new man…Adams felt his anger rising again.

'Shall we begin?' said an imperious voice as the clergyman in question entered the room. 'I have considerable work to do today so I would be grateful if we could keep matters brief. Let us pray.'

The black-clad men sitting around the large oak table bowed their heads and lifted them again almost instantaneously as Vale's brief prayer ended.

'Canon Chancellor, do you have any matters to discuss before we come to the main item?' asked Vale.

Adams cleared his throat and looked down at the papers in front of him on the table.

'You will see from the agenda, Mr Dean, that…'

'I have already said in previous meetings, Chancellor, that an agenda is an unnecessary encumbrance. Perhaps if you would be kind enough to summarise?'

'Very well,' said Adams through gritted teeth. 'There is the matter of the King's Gallery.'

'What of it?' asked Vale blandly.

'The Inspector of the Fabric, and the Clerk of Works, have both issued reports stating that it is unsafe, which is why we have declared it out of bounds.'

'Again, what of it?' repeated Vale.

'You are continuing, Mr Dean, to sit in the gallery.'

'As I understand it, Chancellor,' replied Vale, 'the gallery was made out of bounds to the general public. Not to the officials of the cathedral.'

'But nevertheless, Mr Dean, it is unsafe,' replied Adams. 'And if I may say so, it is also inappropriate.'

'In what way, may I ask?'

'The gallery was constructed for the Allied Sovereign's Visit of 1814, principally for the Tsar of Russia. It was never intended as seating for the clergy.'

'Are you suggesting that it is inappropriate for a man of God to usurp the place of a tyrant?' asked Vale.

There was a chuckle from one of the elderly minor canons, a man called Toddington who was so old and set in his ways that he had not the slightest care over what he said.

'The Russian Tsar would certainly have not appreciated all the bunting and what not you have put up in his gallery, Dean,' said the old man. 'He would have had you sent to the salt mines!' He chuckled again, oblivious to the embarrassed silence of those around him.

'I take it by "bunting" you are referring to the symbols of downtrodden humanity I have placed on the gallery,' said the Dean. 'Symbols of which I am certain the founder of our faith would have approved.'

Adams was tempted to blurt out 'poppycock' but managed to restrain himself. 'If I might continue,' he said calmly. 'Appropriateness aside, I believe it is high time the gallery was removed. We cannot put the public at risk, especially as there have been rumours that persons who object to the flags which the Dean has seen fit to display, may attempt to seize them, and in the process injure themselves.'

Here Adams looked meaningfully at the Dean, but the man was examining his fingernails with a bored expression on his face.

'Then that,' drawled Vale, 'as the common saying has it, is "their own lookout." Is there anything more on this subject?

'As I mentioned in a previous meeting,' continued Adams, 'the estimates for repair for the gallery are very high. But I have recently received a kind offer from a local firm of builders, who are willing to dismantle and remove the entire structure gratis; they ask only to be allowed to retain the timber to sell as firewood.'

There were murmurs of 'seems reasonable' and 'not a bad idea' from the Chapter, but these were cut short by Vale.

'I think not,' he said brusquely. 'Let us continue to keep the public out of the gallery, but allow those members of the Chapter who wish to sit there, to continue to do so. Next item please.'

'There is also the matter of the Chapter servants,' said

Adams. 'Do you, Mr Dean, persist in your desire to relieve them of their duties?'

'I do,' replied Vale. 'Although I prefer to think of it as offering them the opportunity of a fresh start in work more suited to the present day. And I believe there is nothing further to discuss on that topic other than the choosing of the menus for the new refectory, which I hope to present at next week's meeting.'

There were more murmurs. 'Sacking the servants? Preposterous,' and so on. Vale quietened these with a placatory gesture.

'Gentlemen, gentlemen,' he oozed. 'We are called to live simple lives. You can hardly object to that. We are also called to live frugal lives, and this measure will enable considerable money to be saved. Something the Chancellor and Treasurer are always "ragging" me about.'

Dollwood, the Canon Treasurer, a clever but ineffectual man, began to speak, but this time it was the Chancellor who cut him off.

'It's outrageous,' said Adams, his face reddening. 'Some of the staff have worked here for decades. It's not so much that we need them, it's more that *they* need *us*.'

'I find that a rather archaic and almost feudal attitude,' said Vale. 'There is no reason why they may not find work more suitable to our democratic times, once they leave here – with good characters of course.'

There was another chuckle from Toddington, who was looking around the table in amused confusion. 'Does he want us to eat at some sort of soup kitchen, such as those frequented by itinerant labourers? How very novel!'

'An interesting point, Canon Toddington,' said Vale. 'There is nothing novel about it whatsoever. I may often be accused of "progressive" ideas, though *I* am sure I would refer to them as simply humane, but in this case, no conservative can honestly object to a return to the practice of communal meals, which will save money and which has its origins in antiquity.'

'But...but...' spluttered Toddington, looking around for support from the other members of the Chapter; none came.

Bravo, thought Adams sarcastically. Vale is quite the strategist. He wanted to argue, but held himself in check, knowing there was a more important issue at stake. He knew there was very little he could do about Vale.

Under the terms of the cathedral's Royal Entailment, he was answerable only to a clerical court, and Adams knew, from making discrete enquiries, that the men who presided in that court were likely to favour a well-born and well-connected cleric such as Vale rather than someone like himself, who had worked his way up from near-poverty in an obscure Midlands town. All he could do was hope that Vale would see reason.

'If there are no further objections...' said the Dean, in a tone which indicated the lack of objection was already a settled fact. 'Let us then come to the main item of discussion. Canon Chancellor?'

'Thank you Mr Dean,' said Adams. 'As you will all be aware, the cathedral's finances are in a parlous state. Our investments have fared very badly since the slump began and since...that is, in recent times, a number of our benefactors have withdrawn their support.'

There was an awkward silence. Everybody knew why the two or three noble families in the diocese who regularly donated large sums of money had stopped doing so. The Dean might come from the same world as them, but there were some things they simply would not stand for, and the flying of the Red Flag in the house of God was one of them.

'I don't understand,' piped up Canon Toddington. 'Are you suggesting the cathedral has run out of money?'

'Yes indeed, Canon Toddington,' said Adams with a sigh. He knew what was coming next.

'Forgive me, Canon Chancellor,' said Toddington. 'But as you will all no doubt know, I have served this Chapter all my life. I came here in 1880.' He paused, then looked around the table. 'Or was it 1879?'

'It was 1878,' said Adams wearily. 'May we get on?'

'Yes, yes, of course,' said Toddington. 'My point is...now, what was my point...oh yes, my point was, that in those days, the old days, whenever the cathedral needed money, they drew on the funds known as the Carolean Bounty.'

Adams sighed again. 'As I have explained previously, and the Canon Treasurer will corroborate, the Carolean Bounty, namely, the sum endowed on the cathedral by King Charles the Second to support it in perpetuity...'

'...in gratitude for the loyalty of Midchester in the Civil War,' exclaimed Toddington proudly.

'In gratitude for the loyalty of Midchester in the Civil War,' continued Adams with gritted teeth, 'was almost completely depleted by unwise investments carried out by the Canon Treasurer's predecessor.'

'Indeed so,' said the Treasurer, shaking his head sadly.

'To be precise,' said Adams, 'the sum of fourteen pounds, twelve shillings and elevenpence ha'penny is all that remains of the Carolean Bounty.'

'Yes, yes,' said Toddington merrily, who had presumably not heard the exact amount. He raised his hand and pointed upwards like some Old Testament patriarch in a painting. 'We must draw on the Bounty!' The elderly man looked around proudly, as if he had thought of a highly novel idea.

Adams ignored him, and looked instead at Vale, who seemed, as he often did, to be affecting a disdain for what he presumably regarded as the grubby subject of money.

'In short, gentlemen,' said Adams, 'we are facing bankruptcy.'

There was a murmur of disquiet and the Canons looked at each other anxiously, with the exception of Toddington, who was noisily engaged in snorting a large pinch of snuff.

'There may, however,' continued Adams, 'be a solution. I have discussed this with the Canon Treasurer, who has examined the figures and found them satisfactory, and I am sure that when you have heard my proposal, you will all agree with me also.'

Here he looked pointedly at Vale, whose expression of slight boredom did not change; instead he affected to look at his wristwatch and gave a small sigh.

He cannot possibly object to this, thought Adams. The chance to restore the cathedral's finances for decades to come, with no great effort required on anyone's part.

'I have received,' said Adams proudly, 'a most generous offer from a firm of property developers from London.'

There was a murmur of interest. Adams decided to move on rapidly to press home his advantage.

'In short,' he continued, 'the firm has offered to buy Cathedral Farm and some of the smaller neighbouring properties for the sum of sixty thousand pounds.'

A louder murmur of interest this time.

'What on earth do they want it for?' asked one of the minor canons.

'It is, apparently, prime land for development,' said Adams. Can everyone see this?'

He held up a map. 'Cathedral Farm, which as you all know, has been owned by the cathedral since the Norman conquest, is one mile west of here, and covers approximately 100 acres between the new by-pass road and the London and North Eastern railway line. The developers have proposed an estate of several hundred houses of the most modern and well-constructed variety, plus a parade of shops, a cinema, and a temperance hotel. I have also had their assurance that, should we provide the funding for construction ourselves, land will be provided gratis for a mission church.'

'But...' protested Canon Toddington, 'what of the tenants? What were once called the tithes, that is to say, the income from the land? We shall lose it!'

'The income from the land has been pitiful for many years, especially since the slump,' said Adams. 'We will receive far more in interest once it is sold and the money invested. I have informally consulted the farmers and all of them are willing to move without protest.'

'But really,' continued Toddington, 'do we wish to see...suburban villas...on church land? And, and, what was the other thing? Some sort of "temperance cinema"? It sounds utterly ghastly and unfitting.'

'It will all be most respectable, I am assured,' said Adams. 'The land is nowhere near the cathedral so will not affect us in any way. It is a good offer and one which we may not get again if the economic situation continues to worsen. If invested well, the interest from the purchase price should be sufficient to cover all expenses for the foreseeable future.'

There was excited chattering; Adams realised it was time to finish.

'Are we all therefore in agreement?' he asked expectantly.

'No,' came a voice bluntly. It was the Dean.

'I beg your pardon, Mr Dean?' asked Adams, blinking.

'I said no,' said the Dean with a slight smile.

Adams felt anger rising in his chest and fought it down.

'May I ask why?' said Adams.

'You may,' replied Vale. 'And I shall tell you. I oppose the scheme because it is not the function of a cathedral to sell its assets for commercial gain.'

'But there is nothing in law to prevent…' began Adams.

'In the law of man, no,' interjected Vale, 'but in the law of God, yes.'

'Perhaps you would explain,' said Adams, taking a deep breath. He longed for a cigarette, but it was customary for snuff to be the only form of tobacco taken during Chapter meetings, and he disliked the irritating, unsatisfying powder.

'I shall,' said the Dean. 'If we sell off our land for money, we shall be as Esau, selling our birthright for a mess of pottage.'

'What's he talking about pottage for?' asked Toddington of the canon next to him. 'Is he on about the refectory again?'

There were several shushings, and the Dean continued. 'We would be engaging in a shabby commercial transaction of church property purely for monetary gain, to enrich ourselves and these… "property developers".'

'But…' protested Adams, more forcefully this time. The Dean raised his hand in a manner that he was beginning to find infuriating.

'Lest you should think I am simply dismissing the idea out of hand,' said Vale, 'I have an alternative suggestion for Cathedral Farm. I, too, have been making enquiries, and have received a proposal from the Brotherhood of English Workers, for use of the land.'

'The…what?' asked the Treasurer meekly.

'The Brotherhood of English Workers,' said the Dean proudly. 'A communitarian organisation dedicated to the relief of the working poor. They wish to use the land as smallholdings for unemployed mechanical workers from the north of England.'

'And may we know what price they are offering?' asked Adams, although he had a good idea what the answer would be.

'They offer nothing,' said the Dean exultantly. 'It would be a charitable gift by the cathedral to them, and a far better use for it than gimcrack houses for the middle classes.'

'How, therefore,' asked Adams slowly, 'do we solve the problem of the impending bankruptcy of the cathedral and diocese?'

'There is no need,' said the Dean. 'Because I intend that soon there will be no cathedral nor diocese of Midchester.' Here the Dean sat back and folded his arms, as if revelling in his ability to shock.

General uproar ensued. After a silence of sorts had been regained, the Dean continued.

'You must realise, gentlemen, that the cathedral and diocese of Midchester is an anomaly. It has Royal Entailment, and Parliament is seeking to abolish such antiquated privileges of the church – rightly so – and it is far too large and over-manned for an age in which church attendance is in decline.'

The sound of murmuring began again, and the Dean raised his voice.

'I intend for the diocese to be absorbed into the neighbouring administration of St Edmundsbury and for the cathedral to become a simple parish church,' – here the murmuring became an uproar again, and the Dean almost roared his final sentence – 'run plainly and economically with a minimum of expense and with myself as Rector. That will include the selling off of all loss-making auxiliary institutions, including the Choir School.'

Adams could barely believe what he was hearing, and sat silently as the Chapter erupted into angry conversation. This man – born with every privilege life could afford – wanted to wreck what he, a man who came from humble origins, had slaved for years to achieve. And he had the gall to say it was unprofitable when he had managed to broker a deal worth sixty thousand pounds!

'But what of the Bishop?' someone asked plaintively.

What indeed, thought Adams. He pictured the man, a bachelor of the most confirmed variety, sunning himself in some perfumed garden in the Riviera. He was the last hope. Although he had no direct influence in the running of the cathedral, he might at least be able to 'pull strings' somehow.

'The Bishop is approaching retirement and has indicated his willingness to step down,' said the Dean. 'If there are no further questions…'

'The *Arch*bishop…' began Adams, but was cut off.

'The Archibishop and myself see eye-to-eye on the matter,' replied Vale. 'There will be no opposition from the church hierarchy, of that I have made sure.'

Adams, remembering that Vale and the Archbishop were old school fellows, could contain his anger no longer. He stood up, the sudden violent displacement of air sending papers and pens flying to the floor.

'How dare you, sir!' he cried. 'How *dare* you countenance the destruction of an institution that has weathered the storms of nearly a thousand years? Have you no shame?'

The Dean appeared unruffled.

'Kindly calm yourself, Canon Chancellor…' he began.

'I shall not, sir!' expostulated Adams. 'You sit there, pontificating, with your, your ludicrous schemes and supposedly progressive ideas, whilst all the time plotting the closure of this cathedral.'

'The cathedral will not close, Canon Chancellor,' replied the Dean. 'It will merely evolve into something more suitable for the modern age.'

'The modern age!' Adams almost shrieked. 'An age in which it is thought proper for a clergyman to display the symbol of a regime currently engaged in the wholesale slaughter of priests and destruction of churches.'

'If you refer to the flags I have put on display in the gallery…' began the Dean.

'Indeed I do sir, and if I had *my* way they would be torn down! You clearly have no idea of the assaults taking place on our Christian brethren in Soviet Russia.'

'And you, Canon Chancellor,' said Vale, beginning to lose his composure slightly, 'clearly have no idea of Soviet Russia other than from what you read in the gutter press. It is a government of the highest principles.'

Adams began to furiously gather up his papers and stuff them into his briefcase; the other clerics sat in embarrassed silence. When he had finished packing, he stood threateningly close to Vale and spoke calmly and quietly.

'The next time you are standing in the gallery looking down like some medieval prelate, have a care, lest that rotten structure collapse and bring down you and your rotten banners with it. I hereby tender my resignation as Canon Chancellor.'

Vale looked genuinely surprised, and was about to speak, but Adams strode to the door and hurled it open. He turned and raised his voice loudly before stalking out.

'Damn your "highest principles", Vale, and *damn you!*'

Shaw was feeling somewhat mercenary. His lecture to the conference, entitled *Wherever two or three are gathered: the Parish Communion for the smaller church* had been politely received by the delegates, but did not seem to have elicited much interest afterwards.

One cleric had approached him to ask questions, but it seemed the man wanted to talk about Shaw's involvement in a murder case in Lower Addenham. This happened to Shaw from time to time, and he always tactfully brushed off such people, finding them somewhat ghoulish.

He had managed to do so again on this particular occasion, and had returned to Palgrave's house rather than accept the offer of dining with his inquisitor in the cathedral refectory.

If he was truthful with himself, he was only involved in the conference because he was being paid, albeit for a good cause. If he had been asked to speak gratis, he wondered if he would have accepted. He had four more lectures to give over the next four days, and decided that he would keep a low profile the rest of the time; none of the other talks on the programme particularly interested him and he did not wish to have to feign enthusiasm.

As he turned into Cathedral Close he saw a movement at the end of the road, where the Close led out onto the river path. There was somebody there, he was sure this time – a figure in a pale mackintosh with the collar turned up and with a tweed cap pulled down low was walking quickly along the river path from the cathedral. The figure moved furtively, looking behind several times, and then disappeared into a clump of trees near the river.

'What on earth are you staring at, Shaw?' came a voice from behind. It was Palgrave, wearing an academic gown over his tweed suit and clutching a pile of sheet music to his chest.

'Ah, probably nothing,' said Shaw, turning to the organist. 'Might I talk to you inside?'

'Of course,' replied Palgrave, and they entered the little terraced house, wherein Palgrave dumped the pile of sheet music on the table. 'No more lectures today?'

'There is to be a rather tiresome sounding talk on the validity of non-alcoholic wine in the sacraments,' said Shaw. 'I think I shall not attend, but return for Evensong.'

'Sounds wise,' said Palgrave. 'I'm done in already and it's not even lunch-time. The Chapter meeting was somewhat draining – I'll tell you about it later. At least I've got a bit of time off now though. Supposed to be teaching the little ticks in the Lower Fourth this afternoon but they've been allowed to watch the first fifteen play Rendlesham College instead. Our boys are singers first and foremost, not rugby players, so it'll be a bit of a dog's breakfast I'm afraid. Don't want to watch, do you?'

'Not particularly,' said Shaw. 'I have always preferred playing games to watching them, and my rugger days are most definitely over.'

'Jolly good,' said Palgrave. 'I say, how are you fixed for lunch? Aren't your lot dining in the refectory?'

'I thought I might excuse myself from that also,' said Shaw. 'It seems I have something of a reputation among some amateur criminologists there, and I should rather avoid them.'

Palgrave laughed. 'You ought to give a talk on detective methods,' he said. 'It would be much more of a tonic than non-alcoholic communion wine. Good Lord, does anyone other than the Wesleyans seriously propose such an idea? But here's me forgetting my manners. Why not have luncheon with me and Millicent at home? I dropped her a line yesterday saying she might expect us. It won't take us long by bicycle.'

'That sounds splendid,' said Shaw. 'I accept.'

'Righto, I'll get my old boneshaker from the garden and bring it round. Ah, but wait, didn't you want to speak to me about something?'

Shaw paused. 'It is…probably nothing.'

'Do tell, old chap. Problem shared is a problem doubled, and all that.'

'It is not a problem,' said Shaw. 'As I said it is probably nothing, but, have you seen a man, ah, loitering in the vicinity?'

There was a brief moment of silence, and a dark look passed over Palgrave's face.

'Loitering? What sort of man? Where?'

'I did not see his face. He was wearing a cap pulled down low, and a mackintosh. I saw him just now, looking rather furtive near the river, and I am quite certain it was the same fellow I saw by your garden wall last night.'

'Where did he go?'

'Into a clump of trees at the end of the lane.'

'Did he by Jingo? Hmm.'

'I am probably becoming a very suspicious man,' said Shaw. 'But he seemed to be acting in a rather odd manner.'

'Look here Shaw,' said Palgrave warily. 'Let's have a bit of a chat before we leave. If he's who I think he is, I think he's not the sort of chap we want to discuss in front of a lady over luncheon.'

Chapter Four

Shaw and Palgrave pushed their bicycles along the cobbles of the Cathedral Close and then on to the rough muddy path by the river.

'The path is metalled further on,' said Palgrave, 'but we'll have to push for now, unless you want to risk ending up in the drink. It won't take us more than a quarter of an hour or so to get to the ancestral home after we've crossed the ford.'

'A pity there is no bridge,' said Shaw.

'Quite,' said Palgrave. 'I believe some long dead ancestor proposed one in order that he might ride his carriage to services at the cathedral more easily, but what became of his proposal I do not know.'

Shaw cleared his throat. 'Perhaps you might tell me about the figure I saw.'

'Ah yes,' said Palgrave. 'Of course, it may not be the same fellow. But the description – cap and mackintosh – and the furtive manner – ring true enough. We had a little trouble a while back with an undesirable hanging about the choir school, just after I started.'

'Undesirable?' asked Shaw.

'To be blunt, a degenerate.'

'I see. In fact, I do remember something of the sort in the newspapers. No boy was harmed, I seem to recall.'

'No, thank God.' Palgrave looked around warily, and,

seeing there was nobody approaching them on the path, he continued.

'But he was accused of…making improper suggestions, and the police became involved. Nothing was proven. He got three months, I think, and hasn't been back since. But now I wonder…'

'If it could be the same man?'

'Perhaps. I can't see why anyone else would be hanging about like that. I remember the Chancellor got in a blue funk about it being in the newspapers. He was concerned for the boys of course, but hoped it could all be kept under wraps lest the school's reputation be damaged.'

'Can you remember what this man looked like?' asked Shaw. 'In case I should see him again.'

'Hmm,' pondered Palgrave. 'His name was something odd. Peach, that's it. Cyril Peach. He was a low type in appearance as I recall, though I only saw him from a distance when he was arrested outside the cloisters. He wouldn't come quietly, and started making a dreadful racket. Thick spectacles, jowly. About forty, I should say. Sort of chap that looks as if he might be a bit simple, but I think he knew what he was doing all right.'

'Very well,' said Shaw. 'I shall keep an eye out for someone of that description.'

'Right-o,' said Palgrave. He stopped and mounted his bicycle. 'Here's the metalled path. Sis will have luncheon ready. Knowing our luck it will be cold, but still, I'm famished, so let's get a move on.'

Len Skinner dressed carefully in his good suit and a paisley bow tie, and smeared some Three Flowers brilliantine on his hair, combing it back fussily until it had the appearance he desired.

He lit a Craven 'A' cigarette and sauntered downstairs; it was nearly lunch-time and he was looking forward to a pie at a nearby cafe, before beginning the walk out to the racecourse for his weekly debt-settling. He placed bets by telephone, but he preferred to collect the money from the bookmakers in person.

He always walked the two miles or so, unless a pal offered him a lift. He could afford a motor car, but chose not to have one as he did not want to be spotted by the police who would no doubt recognise the vehicle's number plate. A motor car announced you were coming a mile off. No, it was better to go on foot so that he could slip away down a dark alley if he saw a copper, or creep up un-noticed on some tart if she was trying to avoid paying her week's cut.

He tapped on the door of the downstairs parlour, which doubled as the 'boudoir' of Queenie.

The tousled inhabitant eventually emerged, clutching a grubby dressing gown to her mouth and squinting through the haze of the cigarette dangling from her mouth. Somehow, thought Skinner, she seemed less tempting than she had last night.

'Oh, it's you,' said Queenie. 'I thought it might be a gentleman come calling.'

'Well it ain't.'

'Don't I know it, dear. What do you want?'

'A word.'

'Can't it wait? I've a terrible head this morning. That port and lemon I had must have been off. I only had the one.'

'The one gallon. You drink too much.'

'And? You don't expect me to do this sort of work sober

59

do you?'

'You aren't doing any work as far as I can see. That's what I want to talk to you about. Like to earn ten quid?

'Wouldn't I just! Come in then.'

Skinner entered the stuffy room, with its tawdry furnishings and red art-silk scarf draped over the electric standard lamp in the window, now looking dusty and sun-bleached in the late morning light that filtered through the grubby net curtains.

Queenie plonked herself down on the bed, the springs of which squeaked slightly. She patted the faded eiderdown, allowing a small cloud of dust to plume up.

'Sit down dear,' she said, a coy smile on her face.

'No thanks,' said Skinner coldly.

Queenie's smile disappeared and she looked at him with bored expectation. Skinner took a drag on his cigarette, holding it tightly between his thumb and two fingers.

'You ever done any acting?'

'Oh yes,' said Queenie sarcastically. 'Matter of fact Ronald Colman's asked me to play alongside him in his next picture.'

'Straight up?'

'Oh, act your age. I've done a bit of chorus work, and I was a magician's assistant too, until he disappeared in a puff of smoke with a week's rent to pay.'

'Right then,' said Skinner impassively. 'I've got a job for you. If it comes off, we'll both do well out of it. Really well. But you're going to have to convince people that you really like a bloke.'

Queenie laughed with a harsh, grating sound.

'Oh ducks, I've had more than enough practice at *that*.'

Dr Adams stormed out of the Chapter House and strode across Cathedral Green; he felt as if his entire body were driven by an uncontrollable force of anger. Two small boys playing truant from a lesson in the Choir School cowered in front of him on the path with terror on their faces, but he ignored them completely.

It was only when he reached the far side of the Green that he began to slow down and regain some self-control. By the time he reached the Duke of Norfolk pub he was able to stop and catch his breath.

He felt a strange sense of elation come over him, which was not what he had expected at all. A feeling of heavy responsibility lifted. He looked across at the cathedral, and wondered if he might see the raincoated figure again. *Had* it been that benighted man – what was his name – ah yes, Peach – come back to cause trouble again? He rubbed his face. He had no way of telling, and anyway, it was out of his hands now.

Although he had not formally tendered his resignation, there seemed no way he could back down from it. He suddenly had a vision of complete freedom; of living as a simple parish priest in a small church in a remote place. Cornwall, perhaps, on the edge of a rugged cliff. A place where everything that was required could be done with his own hands, from giving Holy Communion to replacing missing slates on the roof.

But then he felt the anger rising in him again at the thought of the Dean and his policy of modernisation. He had relieved the man of the difficulty of having to sack him, for a start. There was more to be done before he disappeared into obscurity, he decided. A little act of revenge.

A few yards away he saw Roberts, the under-organist,

striding towards the cathedral with sheaves of sheet music under his arm. He walked towards him, an idea forming in his head.

'More coffee, Mr Shaw?' asked Millicent, as she played hostess in the drawing room at Mead Lodge. Winnie disliked waiting on tables, and claimed instead to be 'far too busy with the washing up for all that palavar.'

'Thank you but no, Mrs Reynolds,' said Shaw, placing his hand over his coffee cup. 'I ought to be getting back soon; I have a lecture to attend, and then Evensong'.

'I, on the other hand,' said Palgrave, 'am a free agent for the rest of the day. Roberts, the sub-organist, plays on Wednesdays.'

'Staying on for supper, then?' enquired Millicent.

'No, got an absolute pile of marking to get through,' replied Palgrave with a sigh. 'I'd better cycle back with Shaw when he goes.'

'A splendid luncheon, Mrs Reynolds,' said Shaw, as he sipped at his coffee cup. He was not merely being polite; it had been a good meal, he reflected, and yet clearly the result of kitchen economy with some sort of meat that he could not quite identify worked up into a cutlet, with fresh vegetables.

'You'll never guess what it was,' said Millicent, as she puffed on a cigarette and gazed out of the French doors into the garden. 'So I'll tell you. Rabbit, caught by our man Fletcher, and the vegetables were from the kitchen garden.'

'Really Milly,' said Palgrave, who lay in an almost recumbant position on a threadbare sofa while he affected to read a two-day old newspaper. 'Must you make it clear to visitors how low the family fortunes have sunk?'

'Quite frankly yes,' said Milly. 'One ought not to be ashamed of economy and self-sufficiency.'

Shaw smiled at the good natured banter between the siblings, who displayed the sort of close familial relationship that allows frank conversation even in the presence of relative strangers.

'A far better meal than one might find in many expensive establishments,' said Shaw. 'May I smoke?' He raised his pipe, and was met by a nod by Millicent.

He touched a match to the bowl of his Bulldog pipe, and watched Millicent through the wreaths of fragrant smoke that rose up in front of his eyes. She was an odd one, he thought. There was an undercurrent of sadness in her interactions which was entirely absent from her brother. Granted, she was a widow, but she had had many years to adjust to that state. There was something else that Shaw could not quite put his finger on. A sense of being out of place somehow, he concluded.

'I like the smell of a pipe,' said Millicent. 'I always wished Father would smoke one, but he preferred cigars. Good Lord, imagine having to pay for those now. I dread to think what they cost.'

'There you go again,' sighed Palgrave. 'Money. I'm sure Shaw doesn't want to indulge in such vulgarity.'

'Cigars *are* expensive, I agree,' said Shaw. 'Good ones, at any rate. A pipe has always seemed to me a way to enjoy good tobacco without excessive expense.'

'Oh really,' said Palgrave disapprovingly. 'Am I the only one who doesn't care about filthy lucre in this establishment?'

'I wish you would,' said his sister. 'Then perhaps we might not be in such a bind. But I do have an idea of how we might salvage things and keep this place going'.

'Do tell!' said Palgrave excitedly. 'Are you going to marry some American millionaire, with a fortune from corned beef or something?'

Millicent laughed briefly. 'Not quite. I can't say anything at the moment, but as they say in the papers, "watch this space"'.

'You *are* a dark horse, Mil,' said Palgrave, 'but I can tell when your lips are sealed. All right then, I just hope whatever it is comes off because I'm sorry to say things are likely to get rather worse with our finances soon.'

'Oh no,' said Millicent. 'You haven't heard bad news from our stockbroker again, have you?'

'Nothing as profane as that, Milly. No, it looks as if I'll be getting the push.'

'You mean…you are to lose your job?' asked Shaw with concern.

'Can't say definitely, but it looks likely,' said the organist with a sigh as he tossed the newspaper aside and sat up. 'That's what the rather tiresome Chapter meeting today was about. The new Dean's off on one of his modernising frenzies again and he's chopping out the dead wood.'

'But the cathedral must have an organist, surely?' asked Shaw.

'Yes…' replied Palgrave uncertainly, 'but it looks as if the Choir School is going to be shut down, which means I'll have no teaching work, and probably end up as some sort of jobbing organist getting paid two bob a service. I'll probably be better off playing at the local picture palace.'

'But this is preposterous!' exclaimed Shaw. He realised his pipe had become red hot to the touch and resolved to calm his puffing slightly.

'Isn't it?' replied Palgrave. 'Lord, you should have heard the old Chancellor! Told the Dean to go to blazes and said he was resigning. I hope you're satisfied, Milly.'

'What's that supposed to mean?' asked Millicent, who stubbed out her cigarette with a jabbing motion.

'Well, you've always said you approved of the new Dean's methods,' said her brother with a grim chuckle. 'All that progressive stuff, keeping the red flag flying and so on.'

'I said no such thing,' replied Millicent, blushing. 'I merely said he was right about having to look forwards instead of back. Helping the common man, and so on. If that means upsetting a few old dinosaurs who should have retired long ago, then I'm all for it.'

Shaw noticed a frostiness creeping into the conversation, and busied himself with re-lighting his pipe.

'It's a bit more than that, sis,' said Palgrave quietly. 'The Dean's talking about closing half the place down. Turning it into an ordinary parish church. He can do it and there's likely no legal means of stopping him. Sounds as if he's had the go-ahead from the high-ups, too.'

'You mean, we shall no longer have a cathedral?' asked Shaw incredulously.

'Oh we will,' said Palgrave airily, 'but it will be Norwich, or, God forbid, Bury St Edmunds, which isn't a proper cathedral anyway, if you ask me. "Damn you" was what the Chancellor said to the Dean and I can't say I blame him. If looks could kill old Vale would be lying dead in that Chapter House now.'

Skinner drove the Austin 12 saloon slowly along the cobbled street which led towards the back of the cathedral. Queenie was sitting uncomfortably close to him on the front seat.

She wore a hat with a little veil and some sort of fur wrap, and another of her tight dresses, one he had not seen before. It was so tight that he could make out the line of the suspender on her right leg, and he blinked hard and looked away. Come on Len, he thought. Now wasn't the time. If things worked out, well, then maybe. But not now.

He'd borrowed the car from a pal – or what passed for a pal in his world – who owed him a favour. He didn't like the idea but the fact was, there was nowhere else for Queenie to wait and she'd made it clear she wasn't prepared to stand out in the open air. 'Like a common street walker' she'd said, as if, thought Skinner, she was anything else.

'Oh,' said Queenie with distaste, as she dipped her head to look up at the enormous spire of the cathedral. 'That place gives me the shivers. All them dead people lying around.'

'Don't talk daft,' said Skinner. 'When you're dead you're dead.'

'That's what you think,' said Queenie, who turned her attention to the mirror in her little compact, and patted more powder on her already heavily made-up nose. 'I had an old auntie who had The Gift. Second sight, they call it. Used to do your tea-leaves and what not. And *she* said…'

'Oh give over,' snapped Skinner impatiently. Why couldn't women, he wondered, just do the one thing they were worth having around for, and keep quiet the rest of the time? *Christ*, he thought. The idea of being *married* to one of them!

A sonorous tolling began from high up in the cathedral tower.

'Listen,' said Skinner. 'I can hear the bell going faster. That means they'll be starting soon.'

'Here, how do you know that?' said Queenie. 'You

66

haven't seen the light or something dreary like that have you? If you have you've forgotten to bring your prayer book.'

Skinner ignored her, and slowed the car down; he looked around furtively and, once satisfied that there were no policemen to be seen, he brought the car to a halt as near as he could to the vast east window.

'Now, you remember what I told you,' said Skinner, his teeth clenched hard together as he pulled down the peak of his cap and raised the collar of his mackintosh.

'You told me enough times,' said Queenie with a roll of her eyes. 'Lor, I haven't been in a church since mother died. I dare say I might get struck by lightning the moment I set foot inside now, after all the things *I've* done. Why, you've only got to…'

'For God's sake keep quiet, can't you?' hissed Skinner. 'And wait for my signal.'

'Please yourself then,' said Queenie airily, and resumed her cosmetic endeavours as Skinner got out of the car and slammed the door behind him.

'Getting to be a regular jaunt for you two, ain't it, ma'am?' said George, as he led Bounder out of the stables to where Millicent waited in her riding gear.

'Who do you mean?' she asked quickly.

'Why, you and Bounder here of course,' replied George. 'You've been taking him out Wednesday evenings for a few weeks now, 'stead of mornings.'

'Yes,' said Millicent lightly. 'I find he's a bit calmer in the evenings somehow.' She patted the horse's head and he responded with an affectionate shake.

'Well, you'd best enjoy it while you can, I say. Nights are drawing in, and you'll need to go out earlier. You won't want to be riding across the Mead at this time of night come November.'

'Goodness George, why ever not?' asked Millicent. She mounted the horse, with a suppleness of movement which required no mounting block. 'There aren't any highwaymen around anymore you know.'

'Ain't talking about them, ma'am,' said George with a gap-toothed grin. 'It's rabbit holes I worry about. Bounder puts a leg in one of them at the gallop and it's the end of both on yer.'

'Don't be so dramatic,' said Millicent. 'We both know what we're doing. And anyway, I'll be back before dark. Thank you. Walk on.'

She clicked her tongue and Bounder trotted briskly across the yard and through the open gates onto the Mead, where Millicent steered him in the direction of the cathedral.

With any luck, she thought, I shan't need to make this journey for much longer…

Shaw had struggled to remain awake in the afternoon lecture; his late night with Palgrave had shortened his usual eight hours of sleep, and besides, he had to admit that the subject matter – the legitimacy of the use of altar bells in Holy Communion – was somewhat enervating, spoken on at length by a cleric with not only a monotonous voice but also a speech impediment.

It was therefore with relief that he heard the bell ring for Evensong, and before long the conference delegates had filed out from Diocesan House and into the cathedral.

As it was the second service that the delegates were attending, they followed the custom of returning to the seats they had occupied earlier. Shaw smiled; church-going seemed to foster such habits and it looked as if certain cliques within the group of delegates had already claimed particular pews. He was just wondering where to sit, when he heard a voice at his elbow.

'Will you have the same pew again, sir?'

It was the verger who had attended to him at Matins. Shaw nodded, and was led to the little two-seater pew at right angles to the others in the nave. Shaw wondered what the elderly official actually did; there seemed quite a few such characters dotted around at various places doing very little, and he could not help wondering if what the Dean – according to Palgrave's account – had said was true, that there were too many men working in the place.

He dismissed such thoughts as the procession began and the congregation rose to its feet. The choir began the introit, which was William Byrd's *Retire My Soul*. As the ancient phrases rolled and echoed around the vast nave, Shaw felt his vision soften and his breathing become rhythmic.

He had noticed before that cathedral Evensong had this effect on him; the combined beauty of the music and surroundings lulling him into a sort of mild spiritual trance. He looked up and saw that the late afternoon sun, passing through the gently waving trees on Cathedral Green outside, was filtering through the west window and making dancing patterns high up above the altar.

Then came the great liturgy of the Book of Common Prayer, chanted by the Precentor; the cadences and metre of the seventeenth-century language flowing as beautifully as any Shakespearian soliloquy.

The psalm, which was sung by the choir while the

congregation remained seated, was a long one, and seemed to have a soporific effect. The evening was warm, and he noticed one or two heads begin to nod amongst the conference delegates; the elderly verger seated next to him was also fighting against sleep.

He looked along the nave at the congregation; the conference delegates formed a tight-knit group close to the high altar; behind them were the few stragglers that are often found in weekday cathedral services; one or two tourists clutching guidebooks and looking uncertain as to when to stand or sit, a few lonely looking elderly ladies who seemed to know the service by heart, and a serious young man, an undergraduate perhaps, who crossed himself at every mention of the Trinity.

Shaw smiled; these were, he assumed, what were known as 'Evensong Anglicans', people who preferred the anonymity of cathedral worship over that of a parish church. What would happen to such lost souls if the cathedral were to become a mere parish church, with services only on Sundays and perhaps locked the rest of the time? Would there even be a choir, if there were to be no choir school? Where would the Evensong Anglicans get their glimpse of the transcendent?

It was preposterous that the place should change, thought Shaw, as he rose to his feet for the Gloria at the end of the psalm. As he stood he detected a movement above his line of vision; it was Vale, standing high up in the King's Gallery, his hands spread out on the low wooden balcony rail. Shaw felt a twinge of distaste; why was the man not in the choir stalls with the rest of the clergy? Did he think himself literally above everyone else?

There was no sermon, and the service drew to a close fairly quickly. The Prayer for the King's Majesty was truncated and the Prayer for the Royal Family omitted altogether; was this, wondered Shaw, another innovation of the Dean's? He decided such a thought was uncharitable, and devoted himself with gusto to the final hymn, *Lead, Kindly Light.* The dismissal was pronounced by the Precentor and the organ voluntary, a very loud Bach fugue which Shaw recognised but could not name, began to play.

As the crucifer leading the procession stepped forward from the altar, Shaw saw another movement almost outside the top periphery of his vision. He looked up, and saw that Vale was facing away from the edge of the King's Gallery and appeared to be gesticulating or waving; there was a flash of movement next to him, as if a person in light-coloured clothing had suddenly darted forward.

Then, as the organ rose to a crescendo, Shaw, from his unique position facing the gallery, watched in frozen horror as the wooden rail of the gallery gave way. With a barely audible scream, Vale hurtled downwards through space until he landed on the stone floor of the north transept with a sickening thud, which could be heard over the sound of the organ. After what seemed an age, there were three sharp reports as the poles of the three flags affixed to the gallery rail landed on the floor around him.

Shaw sprang to his feet and ran across the nave to the supine body. A thin cloud of blood billowed outwards from Vale's head across the floor, like some ghastly red halo. Even before he reached the body, Shaw knew the man was dead.

Chapter Five

Something approaching chaos ensued once the congregation realised what had happened, but fortunately it did not last long. The under-organist stopped playing abruptly after seeing the commotion on the special mirror set up to enable him to view the nave, and a crowd of people began to form around the body.

Two of the younger vergers, both former military men, took immediate charge of the situation; the choirboys were ushered into the vestry before they could catch sight of Vale's body topped with its blood-soaked surplice, now stained as red as the Soviet flag which lay close by him on the floor.

There were scattered shouts of 'fetch a doctor,' 'is he dead?' and 'telephone for the police.' Shaw, who had been the first to approach the corpse, discretely informed the Precentor that the man was beyond medical help. The Precentor shook his head gravely and a cassock was fetched to cover Vale's remains; the assembled congregation, watching from a discrete distance, needed no further notification of the man's condition.

A strange sense of calm then came over the cathedral and a low hum of conversation began, signifying the beginning of the nervous camaraderie which is often present in crowds following a serious accident. Vergers were appointed to lock the doors to prevent the ingress of the public, and the old verger next to Shaw organised cups of sweet tea from the refectory to give to the pallid elderly ladies in the nave, who were now being fussed over by numerous clergymen, despite their protests that they were 'perfectly all right, thank you' and that they had 'not seen a thing.'

There was then some rather self-conscious throat clearing from the Precentor and mention of a 'a few words of prayer whilst we await the arrival of the authorities'. The 'few words', however, were cut short by the noise of the west door slamming loudly and the sound of metal-segmented boots ringing on the ancient flagstones.

Two ambulance-men, accompanied by several police constables, entered the nave and processed along the aisle, awkwardly removing their head-gear as they did so. The ambulance men gave only a cursory glance at Vale's body, and shook their heads at the police constables, who in turn shook their heads at two men in belted raincoats who had followed them in.

One of the rain-coated men was young, in his mid twenties at most; the other was older but still not yet forty and he had an efficient, brisk air which marked him out as a leader. Shaw surmised from regrettable experience that these were detectives; Criminal Investigation Department men, and sure enough, this assumption was ratified when the older of the two men stepped forward in front of the high altar and addressed the congregation in a loud and somewhat bored voice.

'Gentlemen, and, ah, ladies, thank you for your patience. My name is Inspector Wragg, of the Midchester Police. If you would all be so kind as to return to your places and wait for us to work our way round to take statements, names and addresses and so on, we can let you go on your way. We'll be as quick as we can.'

There was a murmur of conversation as the detective stepped down from the altar; it gradually increased in volume and one or two clerics stepped forward to address the man. He raised his hands in a placatory gesture and spoke even more loudly, almost angrily this time.

'Gentlemen, *please*.' Let us do our job. Yes, I have despatched someone to inform the gentleman's wife. No you are not being held here against your will, but I would greatly appreciate it if you would spare the time to give at least a brief statement as there may be a coroner's inquest. Now please, take your seats and *wait*.'

The murmur of conversation became subdued again and Shaw returned to his pew to wait as the police constables worked their way around the cathedral, taking down the particulars of the congregation.

'I always said that gallery was *unsafe*,' said the elderly verger next to Shaw. 'That is why it was roped off, and a verger placed by the stairs. But the Dean ignored the warnings. His poor, poor wife. Did you see the fall?'

'Yes, quite clearly,' said Shaw. 'Did you?'

'I must confess I nodded off,' said the verger. 'I only awoke once all the commotion started. Oh dear,' he added, 'I shall be of no help to the police.'

Shaw looked across the nave at the various clergyman shaking their heads and pointing towards the altar whilst being questioned by the police constables. Had he, he wondered, due to the unique position of his pew, been the only one to witness the actual fall?

He did not have long to wait. Wragg, the Inspector, wearily dismissed the elderly verger after ascertaining he had seen nothing, and then turned to Shaw, who stood up to face him.

'What about you sir?' asked the policeman. 'I suppose you nodded off as well.'

Shaw could not help thinking the man sounded almost hopeful. He appeared bored by the whole event and seemed impatient to conclude matters as swiftly as possible.

'I am sorry to say I saw practically everything,' said Shaw.

Wragg's eyes widened. 'Good Lord. Maybe there are such things as miracles. You're the first person I've spoken to who didn't spend the entire service either 'eyes front' or asleep.' He looked down at Shaw's pew. 'Then again, I can see yours is the only seat, pew I mean, facing the gallery. I think you might be our star witness, as they say. What did you see?'

Shaw described the fall, and the brief glimpse of what might have been an assailant in the gallery near the Dean.

'Highly unlikely, sir, if not impossible,' said Wragg. 'There's only one way up the gallery, and one of the, what you call them, vergers, was standing at the bottom of the stairs all through the service. He said nobody else went up except the deceased.'

'Could someone have been hiding there?' asked Shaw.

'Eh? Hiding?' replied the Inspector with a grim chuckle, as if Shaw had suggested someone might have been folk-dancing or performing gymnastics in the gallery. 'What on earth for? No, the verger said the gallery was empty. He went up before the service to put the Dean's prayer book out. Made a habit of going up there, so they say, and…here, what's all this anyway? I'm the one asking the questions. What's your name? Where do you come from?'

Shaw felt the man's dark eyes boring into him. He had a sleek, modern face with a slim moustache, and brown hair clipped extremely short at the sides. There was a hint of disdain in his manner.

'My name is Lucian Shaw, vicar of All Saint's church, in Lower Addenham.'

Wragg snapped his fingers. 'I thought so. I don't forget a face easily, and I've seen yours in the paper. You're that parson who's been mixed up in a few murder cases.'

'I have been able to give some small assistance to Chief Inspector Ludd of the Midchester CID in the past,' said Shaw. 'Will he be involved in this case?'

'Case?' asked Wragg tetchily. 'Look here, Mr Shaw. There's no "case" other than a man falling off a wooden balcony that several people have told me was known to be dangerous. There might be an inquest but that's all.'

'I beg your pardon, Inspector,' said Shaw. 'I merely assumed that since the CID was involved...'

'Well don't assume...please,' replied Wragg. 'I'm only here because the station's short-handed and I offered to assist when the call came in. Chief Inspector Ludd is enjoying the last of the sun in Bournemouth on holiday, the lucky so-and-so.'

'And Sergeant McPherson?' enquired Shaw.

'Oh, name-dropping now, are we?' asked Wragg drily. 'McPherson has his work cut out trying to catch a gang pinching things down at the docks. Why?'

'I merely ask, Inspector,' said Shaw carefully, 'because the Dean was known to have antagonised several people. It could perhaps be the case that one of them...'

'Thank you, Mr Shaw,' said Wragg wearily. 'As far as I'm concerned this was just a nasty accident. Don't let your imagination run away with you, eh?' He flipped the pages of his notebook and then paused at a particular page and fixed Shaw with that disdainful expression once more.

'You say you saw a figure in light clothing behind the Dean before he fell, yes?'

'I...think so.'

'Well look around the walls sir. Over there, for example.'

Wragg pointed with his pencil to the high altar. 'Look at that, above the big table thing. Spot of light there, dancing around.'

Shaw looked and indeed there was a flash of white on the stone above the altar, which moved from side to side for a few seconds then disappeared.

Wragg smiled. 'It's caused by the light of the setting sun coming through that big window there,' he said, pointing to the west window. 'There's a tree waving about outside, interrupting the light, like a shadow play. That's most likely what you saw.'

'But…' interrupted Shaw.

'That will be all, sir,' said Wragg with finality, and strode away briskly before Shaw could finish his sentence.

He had been about to point out that there could have been no such flashes of light on the King's Gallery, as the window opposite it faced south, through which there had been no sunshine for several hours.

During the service, Queenie had been sitting patiently in the car but after 20 minutes or so was thoroughly bored, having exhausted every possible cosmetic procedure and smoked all three of her remaining cigarettes.

She idly scanned the dashboard of the vehicle, wondering if it had a built-in wireless. Some of them did, nowadays, she knew, because a gentleman had showed her and told her all about it while he was making nervous small-talk on the drive back to her house. There were knobs in front of her marked 'starter', 'choke', and 'lamps' but nothing marked 'wireless' so she decided it was best not to touch anything in case it broke. That Skinny, she thought, was nice when he was nice, but when he wasn't, well, she didn't want to get on the wrong side of him. The thought of what he might be capable of repelled her and yet somehow intrigued her at the same time.

He was an odd one, she concluded. Any man that successfully resisted her charms, who wasn't clearly a pansy or too old to care, tended to arouse her interest, and Skinner did so in spades.

She knew from talking to other girls who worked for him that he *was* interested in 'that sort of thing', so what was it about *her* that seemed to put him off?

She sighed. Men, she knew from bitter experience, were simple creatures for the most part, but she couldn't work out old Skinny. Him and his plans and schemes. She felt flattered that he had included her in them; did that mean she meant something more to him than his other girls? Jaded though she was, she could not help wondering whether she was falling just a little bit in love with him.

The 'signal' was supposed to be a whistle from Skinner from the graveyard or whatever they called it, at which point she was supposed to get out and follow him as quickly as she could to carry out what they had agreed.

But no whistle came. Instead, she saw Skinner bounding like a race-horse over the low wall which divided the road from the cathedral grounds, his mackintosh fluttering up behind him. There was then a metallic sound as the metal-segmented heels of his shoes skittered on the pavement, and he almost fell into the car through the driver's side door which Queenie had helpfully opened.

''Ere, what you…' she began.

'Shut up talking' hissed Skinner, as he fumbled for the electric starter, 'and keep your head down'.

The engine roared into life and he crunched the gears

briefly before driving off at high speed towards Midchester docks.

Chancellor Adams was still in a state of bleary eyed shock. After the Chapter House meeting had ended he had somehow lost track of all time; all he could remember was that at some point afterwards he had felt a sudden powerful thirst. Realising it was opening time, he had entered an obscure public house deep in a warren of medieval lanes, and had drunk three pints of strong beer in succession.

He looked up in surprise to see one of the sixth-formers from the Choir School in front of him.

'Thank heavens I've found you sir!' gushed the adolescent breathlessly.

'What on earth are you doing here…ah…Treadwell?' asked Adams.

'We had a wager to see who'd find you first. Half a crown's in it for me,' said the boy proudly. 'I say, sir, I couldn't have a glass of beer, could I? I've been looking in every pub between here and School House and it's jolly thirsty work.'

'Certainly not,' said Adams, and Treadwell's face fell.

'Treadwell,' continued Adams wearily, 'would you kindly explain what you are jabbering about? And why you are here? You know perfectly well that public houses are out of bounds to all boys except senior prefects who have reached the age of 18. You, I believe, have not yet attained that privilege.'

'The Precentor gave us special dispensation to go in the pubs, sir,' said the boy. 'And I'm not supposed to tell you why, just fetch you,' he added doubtfully. 'All the Sixth have been sent out to look for you, the whole cathedral's in an absolute uproar.'

'What…what has happened?' asked Adams slowly. 'Come along boy, and tell me instantly, I assure you you will not get into trouble.'

'The Dean's dead, sir,' said Treadwell quietly.

'Dead…?'

'Yes sir. Fell from the King's Gallery during Evensong. I didn't see it, but Cauldwell Minor said that there was blood everywhere, and…'

'Yes, yes, boy, thank you,' said Adams. He felt fear rising in his stomach, and suddenly wished he had not drunk so much ale.

'The Precentor says you've to come straight away to sort things out,' said Treadwell, jabbering enthusiastically. 'He said that, now what was it, something to do with Charles the Second – or was it William the Third – and the cathedral having all sorts of odd rules that have to be kept to. Oh Lor, I *should* know, because I'm hoping to read history at Magdalen next year, assuming I get through that beastly matriculation. Ah yes, that's it: under the terms of the cathedral's constitution, the rules state that…'

Adams interrupted in a whisper. 'That *I* am now Dean.'

It was late evening, and the cathedral and its environs were now hushed. Officialdom had played its brief part and left the stage, leaving no evidence of the day's tragedy except a freshly scrubbed portion of the flagstones in the north transept. Mrs Vale by this time had been informed of her husband's death, and, as a mark of respect, the conference organisers had announced the formal dinner for delegates was to be cancelled; it was a moot point anyway, since the police had still been interviewing people right up to the point when the feast was due to begin. The delegates were left to their own devices and most drifted away from the cathedral to find dinners in the various inns and hotels of the town.

Adams, the new Dean, had been hurriedly installed in a brief ceremony, the form of which had to be found out from a dusty volume in the cathedral's archives, there having been no instance of a Chancellor replacing a Dean through sudden death since 1705.

When the police had left and Vale's body had been removed, Shaw had scribbled a hasty note to his wife and put it in the last post. It was likely that news of the accident in the cathedral would reach her via the morning newspapers and he did not want her to worry.

After a cold collation with Palgrave at the little dining table in his house in the Cathedral Close, the two men sat back and pondered the events of the day. Mrs Snelgrove had reluctantly gone home; she was full of gossip and all sorts of theories about what had happened to Vale and why and had been keen to air them to as many people as possible.

'I rather think old Mrs S has been reading too many tuppenny novelettes,' said Palgrave with a chuckle as he lit his pipe. '*You* don't think the "Angel of Death" pushed him, do you?'

Shaw paused for a moment as he puffed at his own pipe, and slowly shook out a match then tossed it into the fireplace.

'Inspector Wragg thinks it was merely an accident, and seems content to leave it at that,' he said carefully.

Palgrave snorted. 'This Wragg person sounds somewhat

dim, from what I can gather. He seems to want to wash his hands of the whole thing. But I suspect you'd like to find out a bit more.'

'If the police have decided there is no likelihood of foul play,' said Shaw, 'it is not for me to question their decision.'

'Oh come along, Shaw,' said Palgrave. 'How many murder cases have you solved now?'

'I have been privileged to offer some assistance to the police on, let me see, five occasions, but...'

'Don't come the blushing virgin with me, Shaw, it won't wash,' insisted Palgrave. 'You've *solved* five murder cases. Surely you're entitled to express an opinion.'

'I am a clergyman, not a detective, Palgrave,' said Shaw in a tone which indicated the discussion was over.

Palgrave sighed, and blew a wreath of pipe smoke upwards. 'Don't you ever think it odd you've been mixed up in all that lot?'

'Odd?' asked Shaw.

'I mean, don't you think there might be a reason why these things have happened to you? That you just chanced to have been in the vicinity?'

'I believe all things happen for a reason.'

'Quite so. And why, therefore, should it not be that you have been *chosen* in some way as an instrument of the divine will?'

'My dear Palgrave,' said Shaw with a sigh. 'You may be right. But it is not for us to entertain such ideas. To do so would be, I think, a form of pride. The saints did not go about conscious of their sainthood. It is sufficient for us to do our duty in whatever circumstances we find ourselves. To trust and obey.'

'Exactly!' said Palgrave triumphantly. 'So trust and obey your instincts! I can tell you think there's more to this case than the police are saying.'

'You were always able to read me like a book,' said Shaw with a smile, 'and I see that talent has not left you. Yes, I confess I would like to find out more about what happened. And perhaps it would do no harm to make some discreet enquiries in due course. I do think it possible there may have been foul play involved.'

'That's the spirit,' said Palgrave. 'But look here, Shaw, there's no way anybody could have pushed Vale off the balcony. He was on his own up there, the verger verified that. Nobody saw anyone else come or go. *I* certainly didn't see anything, as I was at home catching up with marking the Lower Fourth's miserable efforts at composition.'

'I am not saying there was someone else up there,' said Shaw slowly, 'but I did see *something*. And as far as I can gather, I was the only person in the entire cathedral who actually saw Mr Vale fall.'

'Looks that way,' pondered Palgrave. 'but this, this, figure you said you saw, don't you think the 'tec – what was his name…?'

'Inspector Wragg.'

'Don't you think Inspector Wragg was right, that it was probably a trick of the light?'

'Perhaps. But no direct sunlight was shining on that part of the cathedral – the north transept – at that time.'

'Well, a reflection of some sort perhaps, bouncing off one of the other windows.'

'I think it unlikely.'

'Look here Shaw,' said Palgrave, tamping his pipe tobacco down gingerly with his index finger, 'I think you'd better tell me again exactly what you saw.'

'Very well,' said Shaw. 'I looked up to see Mr Vale standing with his back towards the gallery railing.'

'You're certain it was him?'

'It was a man of his height and build, wearing a cassock and surplice, with a fine head of grey hair. I think we must assume it could have been no-one else.'

'And did you hear anything?'

'No, the voluntary had just started and it was rather loud.'

Palgrave chuckled. 'That under-organist is a bit heavy on the stops sometimes, I agree. Carry on.'

'Mr Vale held his arms aloft in a gesture which appeared placatory.'

'Show me.'

Shaw held up his arms to demonstrate.

'Then what happened?' asked Palgrave.

'He stepped backwards, and appeared to lose his balance; he fell backwards on the wooden railing and it gave way, and he went over, with the flags following him.'

Palgrave winced. 'And this chap you saw…?'

'I confess to not seeing an entire person,' said Shaw. 'It happened very quickly. It was more of an impression of a garment.'

'What sort of garment?'

'Light coloured.'

'A surplice, perhaps?'

'No, not white, but, what is the word, beige, or khaki. Similar to the type of Burberry mackintoshes one had in the war.'

'I know what you mean,' said Palgrave. 'Had one myself. What about his face?'

'I did not see a face,' said Shaw. 'I did glimpse something where a head might be. Perhaps a hat or a cap.'

'You're absolutely certain about this, Shaw? I mean, you don't suffer from spots before the eyes or things of that nature?'

'Never.'

'And you hadn't nodded off like old Liversedge – the verger – next to you on the pew. I mean, you didn't dream it?'

'Certainly not.'

'Hmm.' Palgrave tapped his pipe out briskly on the little brass ashtray on the table in front of him. 'Very well, let's consider what we know so far. It sounds as if a person unknown, wearing a mackintosh and cap, somehow got into the King's Gallery without being seen and managed to push Vale off it, and then somehow got away without being seen as well.'

'I did not say for certain,' replied Shaw, 'that Mr Vale was pushed, I said that he appeared to fall backwards.'

'But why would he step back so suddenly like that?'

'He had his hands in the air,' said Shaw. 'I wonder if…'

'A "stick-up"!' cried Palgrave excitedly.

'Come again?' asked Shaw.

'A "stick-up". That's what they call it in the American films. A chap pulls out a pistol and everyone's hands go up. "*Hande Hoch*", as they used to say in the war, not that I ever took a prisoner, mind. But it's a natural instinct to throw one's hands up like that when confronted with a gun.'

'Very well,' said Shaw. 'Perhaps a man with a pistol threatened Vale for some reason, he stepped back and then fell to his death, and the man escaped somehow.'

Palgrave appeared deep in thought, then punched a fist into his palm. 'A cap and mackintosh, you say?'

'Something of that sort.'

'But dash it, Shaw, that's what that fellow you saw hanging around the cathedral close was wearing. Do you think there might be a connection?'

Shaw finished his own pipe, and cleaned it out with the

little knife he carried for that purpose.

'Perhaps...'

Before he could continue, Palgrave interrupted. 'And if the man you saw *was* that fellow, er, Peach – the one that was had up for indecency, perhaps he had a grudge against the Dean, and...'

'I think we should not jump to conclusions,' said Shaw. 'We have no evidence the man I saw was Peach. Did Mr Vale have any enemies?'

Palgrave laughed. 'Dozens, especially after he put those flags up in the nave. One of the newspapers called him 'England's most hated clergyman' and was running a campaign to have him defrocked. Why, he even had threatening letters sent to him.'

'What sort of letters?'

'Oh, you know the sort of thing,' said Palgrave. 'Vale passed them round in Chapter meetings. Seemed to think it was all great fun. Ex-military types, most of them. "You blank blank so-and-so, how dare you display the flags of Indian mutineers and Fenians in the House of God," etcetera. He said such hatred and what he called "bigotry" only served to convince him he was right to put those flags up.'

'So,' mused Shaw, 'a disgruntled or perhaps even unbalanced former soldier, with access to firearms, might be a possibility. But what about more local enemies?'

Palgrave laughed again. 'You heard what he was like. I think all of us probably wanted to see him dead at one time or another. Look here, you're not putting this in some notebook are you? I don't want people getting the wrong idea.'

'I am merely assessing possibilities,' said Shaw. 'Let us consider them. Vale was threatened, or at least in some way surprised, by an unknown person. He may have been pushed, or simply lost his balance and fell to his death. The verger, and we have no reason to doubt him, says that nobody else was on the balcony before the service, and nobody apart from Mr Vale could have gone up or down without being noticed.'

Palgrave smiled. 'What's that line from the Sherlock Holmes stories? "When you have eliminated the impossible, whatever remains, however improbable, must be the truth."'

'I am not very familiar with Mr Conan Doyle's works,' said Shaw, 'but it strikes me that, clever as that quotation sounds, it does depend on one's interpretation of the word "impossible"'.

'I say, Shaw, that's a very good point,' said Palgrave. 'It's impossible, of course, for a man to appear and disappear from a balcony without anyone seeing him. But what if...'

'What if Mrs Snelgrove is right, and it was not a man, but some sort of supernatural visitation?' asked Shaw. 'Is that what you mean?'

'I must admit I did wonder,' said Palgrave. 'It seems incredible, but, well, the Christian religion is full of incredible things. Divine messengers, and so on.'

'Divine messengers that hurl clergymen from balconies, as punishment for their progressive views?' asked Shaw with a raised eyebrow.

'Well...' replied Palgrave doubtfully, 'I don't say such things *can't* happen...'

'Nor I,' said Shaw. 'But I think it extremely unwise, and intellectually lazy, to rely on supernatural explanations simply because all rational ones seem to have failed. God moves in a mysterious way, as the hymn tells us, but He appears to do so mainly via human agency.'

'The Age of Miracles has passed, and all that, eh, Shaw? said Palgrave. 'I'm a musician, not a theologian, but I take your point. There may well be a logical explanation as to how a potential assailant got on and off the balcony without being seen, but I'm hanged if I know what it could be.'

'I think there may be a very simple explanation,' said Shaw, 'and with your help I may be able to prove it.'

Chapter Six

'Is everything all right, ma'am?' asked Winnie as she cleared away the breakfast things in the sepulchral drawing room at Mead Lodge.

'Only Mr Fletcher says as you looked right peaky when you came back from your ride yesternight. Said you looked as if you'd seen a ghost.'

Millicent paused, and pushed away the bowl of porridge from her place on the table. 'Only cads eat porridge sitting down', her father had said, claiming it was a meal to be eaten standing up while waiting to be called at any minute for the start of a hunt. Well, father was long gone as were the large hunt breakfasts at the Lodge, and so the point of protocol was moot; she could not possibly afford such hospitality now.

'I said is everything all right?' repeated Winnie, looking with concern at Millicent.

'I'm sorry, I was miles away,' said Millicent. 'Yes, I'm perfectly all right thank you, Winnie. I was…just a little tired last night. Riding seems to do that to one sometimes.'

'I'm sure I wouldn't know, ma'am,' sniffed Winnie. 'You wouldn't get me sitting on one of *those* things. Horses is for men, if you ask me, and nowadays they don't even need them as they all have motor cars and motor bicycles, and what have you.'

'As I can't afford a motor car, and loath bicycles, I shall

have to make do with Bounder,' said Millicent with a weak smile. 'Was there anything else?'

'Oh yes,' said Winnie excitedly. 'I almost forgot. You've heard the news?'

'About what?'

'The Dean of Midchester.'

Millicent paused before answering. 'What about him?'

'He's dead!' said Winnie with relish. 'Died last night. It made the morning paper, just a little bit, like, but I heard it first from the dairyman, who delivers to the Cathedral Close afore he comes here.'

Millicent bit her lip and there was another pause.

'How…did he die?'

'Broke his neck,' answered Winnie with enthusiasm. The violent death of somebody unknown personally to her was something to be treated with as much enthusiasm as any other piece of gossip or scandal.

'It's all in the paper,' said Winnie proudly, taking a copy of the *East Anglian Daily Times* from her apron pocket and carefully unfolding it as if it were holy writ. She jabbed her finger at a small article at the bottom of the front page.

Millicent read the headline quietly out loud. '"Dean dies in fall. The Very Reverend Eckhart Vale, Dean of Midchester Cathedral, died yesterday evening after falling from a balcony during Evensong…"'

Her voice trailed away and she arose from the table with a start.

'Here, you've gone pale again,' said Winnie with concern. 'If you're upset about that Dean, I wouldn't worry about *him*,' she added. 'From what I've heard, he was a rum 'un. A Red, so they say. Now what on earth a parson wants to be one of *them* for I don't know. If you ask me….'

Winnie stopped talking and gazed in bewilderment as

Millicent hurried out of the room, clutching her handkerchief to her mouth.

Shaw had just finished delivering his morning lecture, entitled *Holy Communion at the last*, about the administration of the sacraments to those on their deathbeds. He had spoken with a certain lack of enthusiasm. The topic could hardly be more pertinent and yet somehow it seemed distasteful.

He wished that Vale had been able to partake of such a comfort, but it had been too late. He thought of a half-remembered line of poetry whose author he could not remember either. 'Betwixt the stirrup and the ground, I mercy sought, and mercy found.'

Had Vale found mercy in those few seconds as he tumbled through space? How terrible, thought Shaw, to be so suddenly and violently called before one's maker. Granted, the Dean had died during divine service, after the General Confession and Absolution, but still...

Shaw heard the discreet cough of the chairman who thanked him and announced that refreshments would be served in the refectory. Shaw stepped down from the lectern and joined the general throng.

There seemed to be an air of distraction among the conference delegates, and the conversation over tea was noticeably more subdued than previously.

'Thank you, Mr Shaw, for an interesting talk,' came a voice from beside him in the crowd. He turned to see Dr Adams.

'I regret we have not been formally introduced,' said the new Dean, 'but there seems nobody around to perform the task and I have very little time. We are all rather shocked and there is a great deal to organise.'

'Good morning, Canon Chancellor,' said Shaw. 'I did not realise you were among the delegates.'

'I thought in my new role I ought to make an appearance,' said Adams. 'And it's "Mr Dean" now, rather than Canon Chancellor,' he added.

'Ah, yes, of course,' said Shaw. 'My apologies, Mr Dean.'

'No need to stand on ceremony. '"Dr Adams" will suffice.'

'Very well. I had forgotten the investiture took place so quickly.'

'Oh, I have not been invested yet,' said Adams. 'That will not take place until the Bishop returns from wintering abroad. But it is one of this cathedral's many peculiarities that, in the absence of an appointed successor, the Chancellor succeeds the Dean the moment he dies. There is no interregnum, in just the same manner as the throne of England passes immediately to the heir apparent upon the death of the sovereign.'

'I confess to being no expert on cathedral traditions,' said Shaw. 'The small country parish is my field of expertise, such as it is.'

'Come come, Mr Shaw,' said Adams genially, leading him gently through the throng to a quieter corner of the refectory. 'I think we both know you have another field of expertise. Your detective work.'

Shaw bridled slightly, but tried not to show it. 'I am a country parson, Mr Adams. That is all.'

Adams laughed, in a way that Shaw thought somewhat inappropriate given recent events. 'Just *a povre persoun of a toun*, as Chaucer put it, eh? Did you know he passed through here, in 1370, on his way to the shrine at Walsingham? There's a record of him giving fourpence to the alms house. So you're not the first famous person we've entertained at the cathedral.'

'I very much hope I am *not* famous,' said Shaw firmly.

'Perhaps not in the way of Chaucer,' said Adams, 'but sufficiently well known to attract attention from the press. Your attendance was already mentioned in the *Church Times* before the conference began and I suspect it helped with what the Americans call "publicity".

'Then perhaps I ought not to hide my light under a bushel,' said Shaw somewhat reluctantly. 'Anything that helps raise money for the church is a good thing.'

'That's the spirit,' said Adams. 'Now, have you any theories?' he asked quietly.

'About what?'

'About the death of the late Dean. From what I gather, you were the only person to see what happened.'

Shaw felt he was being pumped for information, and resented it. There was something about Adams he did not like; his ruddy geniality somehow rang hollow and did not quite mask an underlying air of pomposity. He decided to be as taciturn as he could whilst not offending the man. After all, he thought, I may need to speak to him again.

'I read a brief account of the accident in this morning's newspaper,' said Shaw. 'The gallery rail was rotten, and could have given way at any time, and therefore the police are satisfied it was an accident.'

'That's all very well, but what do *you* think?' asked Adams.

Shaw smiled. 'If that is the opinion of the police, then I wholeheartedly respect it. Now, if you will excuse me, Dr Adams…'

'A politician's answer, eh, Shaw?' said Adams with a wry smile. 'All right, I won't interrogate you any further. But if you *do* come up with any theories, you let me know, eh? I've a right to know what's going on. After all, it's *my* cathedral now.'

Skinner had had a sleepless night; the half-bottle of whisky he had consumed had seemed only to make him more wakeful. He had made a half-hearted attempt to wash and dress, and was now reviving himself in his squalid back kitchen with a Capstan cigarette and a pot of tea.

He had to think. After what had happened at the cathedral last night, ought he even to stay in Midchester? He was known to the police, but they had never managed to pin anything on him yet because he was careful. There was no law against having women lodgers in his house, and the little bookmaking club he ran in the back room of the local pub always had a look-out posted in case the coppers came nosing around, which they never did round that part of town because they knew what was good for them.

Perhaps it was time to move on. If anyone had seen him – and Queenie – then it could be curtains. Could he trust her? She hadn't *seen* anything, that was true, but she knew what he'd been planning. And now…

His thoughts were interrupted by a crash at the front door; he jumped up and instinctively reached for the razor in his trouser pocket. He then slumped back into his chair when he realised what the noise was.

He walked through the dingy passageway to the front door and picked up the newspaper that had just been pushed through the letterbox. Late again; the local newsagent had apologetically told Skinner he found it almost impossible to get reliable paper boys. It made the same noise every morning, but he was so on edge today that he had, for a brief moment, imagined it was some copper's size nine boot kicking in the door.

Skinner lit another Capstan and scanned the headlines on the front of the paper. He saw the article about the death in the cathedral and almost wept with relief when he read the words 'the police are not treating his death as suspicious.'

From nearby in the front parlour he heard the sounds of Queenie turning in her bed and yawning. He caught a brief hint of her perfume through the door, and felt an unexpected flood of desire mingled with the sense of relief. He suddenly thought, why *not*?

Without knocking, he let himself into Queenie's room and bolted the door behind him.

Shaw related his conversation with the new Dean to Palgrave, as the two took elevenses in the Cathedral Close. Palgrave had a free period from the choir school, and Shaw had decided not to attend the morning's second lecture, entitled *Incense and the small church: some practical considerations.*

'I heard something rather odd about Adams this morning, as it happens,' said Palgrave, as he stuffed some London Mixture into his pipe and then lit it.

'It appears,' he continued between puffs, 'that he met Roberts, my sub, on Cathedral Green yesterday after storming out of Chapter, and told him to change the voluntary I'd specified for Evensong.'

'Why should the music played at the end of the service concern the Chancellor?' asked Shaw as he sipped his tea.

'Particularly if he had already tendered his resignation.'

'Well exactly,' said Palgrave. 'The thing is, what aroused my interest was *what* he asked Roberts to play.'

'Something by Bach, I think?'

'Correct. To be precise, it was *Der tag der ist so freudenreich.* Which if my German is correct, means something along the lines of "this is the day of rejoicing".

'What is unusual about that?' asked Shaw. 'Bach is often played as a voluntary.'

'Yes but we don't usually have a piece like that,' said Palgrave. 'Have a listen.'

Palgrave strode to the piano and sat down. 'Vale couldn't abide loud or jolly voluntaries at Evensong and specifically forbade myself or Roberts from playing them. He thought the end of the service should be reflective, and always asked for quiet pieces.'

'Did he have right of veto over you?' asked Shaw.

'Oh, Lord knows,' said Palgrave. 'Apparently there was some bye-law from the year dot that said he could dictate whatever music was played, I remember having a bit of a spat about it with him and I eventually had to back down. He always wanted things like this.'

With his pipe clenched between his teeth, Palgrave's long fingers fluttered over the keys and effortlessly produced from memory the opening bars of the Bach *Passion Chorale.* Shaw was transfixed, and realised he had never seen Palgrave play before; there had been no opportunity, of course, on the Western Front. How was it such hands had been trained to produce such beauty, he wondered, but had also been trained to kill his fellow man?

He was woken from his reverie by Palgrave suddenly transitioning into a different piece of music which was upbeat, almost jaunty. His head swayed from side to side, and little flecks of ash flew from his pipe, which he deftly flicked away from the keyboard without missing a note.

'Now this is what Roberts played last night,' he said, raising his voice to make himself heard. 'Can you hear the difference?' The piano shook from the cascade of chords and myriad individual notes that poured forth from beneath its open lid.

'It's loud enough on the piano,' shouted Palgrave, 'but on the organ it needs both manuals and the pedals, with nearly all the stops out, including the Great Trumpets. It's *fortissimo* and goes into triple *forte* at the end, making it sound as deafening as a blasted fairground ride.'

Suddenly there was silence as Palgrave stopped playing. He removed his pipe from his mouth and folded his arms.

'It's usually played at Christmas anyway,' he said, 'and we're weeks away even from Advent. Now why,' he asked, 'do you think Adams asked for that?'

Shaw thought for a moment. 'Did Dr Adams have a right of veto over Mr Vale in matters of music?' he asked.

'That wasn't the response I was expecting,' said Palgrave, 'but good point, Shaw. I don't think he does, or rather did, have any veto, but Roberts is a delicate flower and told me that Adams looked so incandescent he thought he'd better do what he said.'

'Very well,' said Shaw. 'My assumption would be that Dr Adams simply wanted to annoy the Dean, and it was a last act of petty revenge. Perhaps the title itself was a dig at him. The man was rejoicing at having resigned.'

'Hmm, but don't you think there could be another reason?' asked Palgrave with a quizzical gaze in Shaw's direction.

'Such as?'

'Do come along, Shaw. I'm doing all your work for you. If some cove wanted to push some other cove off a balcony without being heard, wouldn't it make sense to do so whilst a very loud piece of music was being played?'

'You are suggesting,' said Shaw slowly, 'that Adams had some involvement in Vale's death?'

'Not just "some involvement",' said Palgrave. 'Remember that Adams had it in for Vale and had just had a blazing row with him. I'm saying he might actually have done it himself.'

'Last night you said you could not understand how anyone else could have been in the balcony to do such a thing,' replied Shaw.

'And I still don't quite understand,' said Palgrave, as he briskly shut the piano keyboard lid. 'But I suggest we use the rest of our free time to visit the scene of the crime and find out how. And if it *was* possible for someone to be up there without being seen, I rather think old "Angry Adams" is our number one suspect, don't you?'

'I think that's all the loose ends tied up, as they say, madam, so I shan't need to trouble you further. Thank you for the tea.'

Inspector Wragg replaced the half-drunk cup of tea in its saucer and stood up.

'Thank you, Inspector,' said Mrs Vale with cold formality. She was dressed in deepest mourning, her black dress off-set by some discreet antique jewellery. 'I would ring for the maid to show you out, but we are rather bereft of domestic help. My husband rather disapproves – disapproved – of too many servants about the place.'

'That's quite all right, madam,' said Wragg. 'I'll see myself out. I dare say our paths will cross again if an inquest is called, but having spoken to the coroner this morning it looks as if he is as satisfied as me that it was all an unfortunate accident. '

'So you have said,' replied Mrs Vale.

'I'll inform you in a day or so in order that you can make funeral arrangements,' he added. 'And…ah…I suggest you wait until the undertakers have had a chance to, er, before you view your husband's body, that is, a chance to…'

'To clean him up?' asked Mrs Vale briskly. 'I am under no illusions as to how he died, Inspector,' she added. 'But thank you for the warning.'

There was a pause and then Wragg cleared his through. 'Nice house, this,' he said, as he looked around, holding his hat awkwardly as if unused to such venerable surroundings.

'Yes, but I shan't be here much longer, of course,' replied Mrs Vale. 'Dr Adams, the new Dean, will be moving in as soon as possible, if I know *him*. I expect some sort of grace-and-favour cottage will be made available. My husband's people are quite well off, and can doubtless afford to keep a poor relation.'

'Stand to inherit a lot, do you, madam?' asked Wragg.

'I fail to see the relevance of that question,' said Mrs Vale coldly, 'but I shall be comfortable. One ought not to ask for more in this mortal life.'

'Ah…quite,' said Wragg uncomfortably. 'These yours, are they?' He pointed with his hat to a bookcase which contained two rows of detective novels with gaudy dust-jackets.

'They help pass the time.'

'I see. I ask because I wondered if like some others I've interviewed, you might think that your husband's death might not have been accidental.'

'Inspector,' replied Mrs Vale, 'it is your job to investigate and I leave it entirely in your hands. I fail to see any connection with my reading habits.'

'Remember one thing, madam,' cautioned Wragg. 'Remember those books are just stories. Real life – real crime, I should say, isn't a bit like them. A person can make life very difficult for himself if he starts imagining things about plots and schemes and what-not.'

Mrs Vale stiffened. 'I am quite capable of distinguishing between fiction and reality. I think I *shall* ring for the maid. She may as well earn her keep.' She made a move to the bell-push by the chimney-piece.

'I, ah, didn't mean to refer to *you*, madam,' said Wragg somewhat awkwardly. 'It's just that the craze for detective fiction has got everyone thinking they can do a better job than the police. Take this chap Shaw, for example.'

'Who?' asked Mrs Vale distractedly as she pushed the bell to summon the domestic.

'Reverend Shaw, madam. A parson, from one of the villages a few miles away. He likes to think of himself as an amateur sleuth, and has poked his nose into a couple of murder cases. My superior, that is, Chief Inspector Ludd, has had to help him out when he's run into difficulties. He's here for the conference, and Lord, he tried a theory on me that your husband's death was, well, let's say, suspicious – but *I* told him I wasn't having it.'

'I have heard something about him, I think,' said Mrs Vale. 'He's a friend of the organist, I believe.'

'That's right, madam,' said Wragg. 'Staying here for a few days. I told him…'

The Inspector was interrupted by the arrival of the maid.

'Would you show the Inspector out?' said Mrs Vale.

Wragg mumbled his farewells and was shown out. Mrs Vale went to a bureau in the corner of the room, and after a few moments, found what she was looking for.

'The constables have given strict instructions that nobody is to be allowed up, sir,' said the verger to Shaw and Palgrave as they stood at the foot of the metal spiral staircase which led to the King's Gallery.

'Of course, of course, Pettigrew,' said Palgrave blithely. 'But they were referring to the general public, no doubt. Not members of the Chapter.'

'Well…I…that's as maybe sir,' replied Pettigrew doubtfully, 'but I don't know as I recognise this gentleman with you. He's not one of the Chapter.'

'No, but he's with me,' said Palgrave. 'You've heard of Reverend Shaw, of course.'

Pettigrew's formerly obstructive tone seemed to soften a little. 'Ah, the gentleman from Lower Addenham who solved that killing in the village hall a couple of years ago? My cousin, or rather my wife's cousin, lives in Addenham and she told me all about him.'

'How do you do, Mr Pettigrew?' said Shaw, shaking the man's hand warmly. 'Who is your cousin?' he added with a smile, seeing an opportunity to get the man on his side.

'That'll be Bessie Burgess, sir,' said Pettigrew.

'Of the cake shop, I think? Her bath buns are the pride of the village.'

'That they are, sir,' said Pettigrew with a chuckle. He turned to Palgrave. 'I suppose it'll be all right if you go up. But watch that broken railing. We don't want another death, God forbid. Is Mr Shaw helping the police with their enquiries, as they say?'

'Not officially,' said Palgrave. 'Thanks awfully Pettigrew. We'll only be a minute.'

Shaw followed Palgrave up the steep staircase and after what seemed an age, they finally reached the wooden gallery which spanned the enormous vaulting of the north transept at approximately the roof level of a two-storey house.

Shaw recoiled slightly as he realised how high they were, and how low the wooden railing was in front of the two rows of pews facing it. He looked gingerly over the rail, and saw a few straggling tourists milling around, and a crocodile of visiting school-children who appeared doll-like from such a distance. He resolved to keep well away from the broken section of railing whence Vale had fallen, and walked across the creaking floorboards to relative safety where the balcony joined the north wall.

'Do you know I've never been up here?' said Palgrave. 'No reason to really. I had no idea it goes back so far.'

'The cathedral guidebook, which I purchased when I arrived for the conference,' said Shaw, 'states that it is some forty feet square. It covers almost the entire north transept.'

'What on earth did they need all this space for?' asked Palgrave as he wandered around. 'Something to do with the Russian Tsar, wasn't it?'

'Quite so,' said Shaw. 'According to the guidebook it was built for the Allied sovereigns' visit to England in 1814. It was built supposedly at the request of King George the Third, hence its name.'

'The mad one, eh?' said Palgrave. 'No wonder. It's a dashed silly piece of work if you ask me. I suppose the idea was to celebrate the defeat of old Bonaparte, eh?'

'It seems so. The entourage, which included the Russian Tsar and the King of Prussia, had been due to attend a service of Evensong following a visit to Cambridge, in order to break the long carriage journey back to London.'

'But why on earth build all this thing?' asked Palgrave. 'Why not just sit them in the nave? Even the Prince of Wales had to put up with that when he visited last year.'

'Remember that sectarianism was far worse in those days,' said Shaw. 'The common people of Midchester objected to the visit, and there were fears that mob violence might break out. There were no police constables to keep order.'

'But the Tsar was on our side in the war!' expostulated Palgrave.

'Yes,' replied Shaw, 'but he was of the Orthodox religion. In the minds of the ordinary folk of the day, that would have been no different to a Papist. They would not abide his presence at a Protestant service and there were fears of violent disorder. Hence the gallery was built in order to make sure the visitors could be protected.'

'My goodness, what a lot of fuss – and expense,' said Palgrave.

'Indeed,' replied Shaw, 'and it was not even, in the end, required. The party apparently returned from Cambridge directly to a ball in London.'

'And so the bally thing has sat rotting away here ever since,' said Palgrave. 'Adams had an offer by a local firm to have it taken down free of charge, but Vale blocked it. I think he saw it as a roundabout attempt at getting his red flag taken down.'

'It seems to me,' said Shaw with regret, 'that nothing good comes of clergy embracing modern political fashions.'

'Old Vale, God rest his soul,' said Palgrave, 'seemed to think that Our Lord would have been a Bolshevik if He had been around today.'

'Well, well,' said Shaw with a sigh. 'It is not for us to speculate. We are here, after all, to find out what happened

103

to the late Dean.'

'Of course,' said Palgrave. 'I'll stop jabbering. I've noticed one thing already.'

'Which is?'

'That section of the balcony over there, towards the altar. There's a chair there, tucked away. Now what's that all about?'

'I noticed that when we came up,' said Shaw. 'But did you notice anything about its position by that pillar?'

The two men walked over to the chair, which was of the plain wicker-seated type used in the nave.

'I say,' said Palgrave. 'It can't be seen from the nave. Whoever sat in it would be invisible to anyone downstairs.'

'Quite so,' nodded Shaw. 'I have looked up at the gallery from the nave from several angles, and I did not once notice it.'

'So somebody could have been up here during Evensong,' said Palgrave enthusiastically. 'He could have sat up here and then pushed the Dean over and...' His face fell. 'No, that wouldn't work. For a start, Pettigrew swore blind nobody was up here before the service because he checked beforehand.'

'Indeed,' replied Shaw.

'And,' continued Palgrave, 'if it were somebody who wished to do the Dean a mischief, why, the old boy would have seen him the moment he set foot on the balcony. He could hardly have crept up from behind and pushed him over. Unless...unless of course it was somebody he *expected* to be there.'

'That is still not a possibility,' said Shaw, 'if we are to believe Mr Pettigrew's account. And as you say, we have no reason to disbelieve him.'

'You don't think he nodded off, or something, do you,

and allowed someone to creep past him on the stairs?' asked Palgrave with a hint of desperation.

'Pettigrew was standing up during the entire service,' said Shaw. 'He could not possibly have fallen asleep. The stairs were in my line of vision also, and I would surely have seen somebody attempting to climb them. It would have been quite noisy; those steps are metal and would make something of a din.'

'Oh hang it all Shaw,' said Palgrave with exasperation. 'I think we're on a wild goose chase. Perhaps Vale *did* just fall off by accident after all, and what you saw behind him really was just a trick of the light.'

'There is another possibility,' said Shaw.

'Not one of Mrs Snelgrove's phantoms rising up out of the floorboards, surely? Bad show, Shaw. That's what a classicist would call a *Deus Ex Machina*. It won't wash I'm afraid.'

'"There are more things in heaven and earth than are dreamt of in your philosophy", Palgrave,' quoted Shaw with an enigmatic smile. 'However, what I propose is something rather more mundane than a ghost. Come and look at this.'

Chapter Seven

Millicent had ridden for miles and no longer knew, nor cared, where she was. Bounder steamed and sweated beneath her, and she was suddenly brought to her senses when he shook his head in violent protest at the pressure of the bit in his mouth.

She slowed the horse to a trot and then a walk, and finally they stopped by a ridge overlooking a long sweep of farmland which led down to a wide shingle beach and then the vast grey-blue expanse of the North Sea, as calm as a village pond on this fine autumnal day, which was almost as warm as high summer.

To her left, the estuary of the River Midwell meandered and twisted like a vast shimmering serpent on its slow journey to the sea, and on it she could make out the red sails of the Thames barges making their slow way around the coast from London.

London...could she escape there, she wondered? She had little knowledge of it. Since she had married young, and in the midst of war, there had been no formal *debut* or London season for her, and after that, only the quiet life of a young widow in the country. Abroad, then. Paris perhaps? But her French was poor, and it would be difficult for her to blend in; if she met with any English people, they would be sure to notice her and ask questions.

As she gazed out to sea, she seemed to glimpse all of the

European coastline stretched out in front of her, from the pine-covered wilderness of the Baltic to the sunlit rocks of the Aegean. And beyond, the endless enormity of the East: the Levant, India, and the Orient. For a moment it seemed she could go anywhere, do anything…but then, a cloud crossed the sun and she shivered slightly.

It was hopeless, she thought. And not only that, it was cowardice too. The police had not called today, but they would soon. 'Not treating the death as suspicious', the papers said, but that could be a ruse to get her to let down her guard. Surely they must come. Perhaps even now, detectives were watching railway stations and ports for her, and clipped, expressionless voices were describing her on wireless bulletins.

She had another vision, of men in khaki uniforms and solar topees; armed men, arriving to arrest her in some dark, steaming outpost of the Empire to which she had been hounded, like the poor foxes she had once thought nothing of chasing to their doom.

She decided she must stay and face them. Until then, she would act as if nothing had happened. But when they came, it would all have to be told. She ran her hands through her hair; she had come out hatless, unable to find the cap she usually wore while riding, and too upset to think logically about where it could be. Suddenly, with a cold feeling of horror, she remembered where she might have dropped it.

'A secret passage?' expostulated Palgrave. 'Come along, Shaw. Isn't that all rather *Castle of Otranto?*'

'Perhaps,' said Shaw, who was running his hands along

107

the Georgian timber panelling between the King's Gallery and the east wall of the transept. 'Such things do exist, particularly in places frequented by important personages.'

'You mean,' replied Palgrave slowly, 'something built so that the Tsar and his entourage could make a quick escape if the local populace cut up rough?'

'It certainly seems odd to build such a balcony with only one entrance and exit,' said Shaw, as he peered closely at the grey-green paint on the woodwork of the panels, pockmarked and peeling with age.

'And I recall,' he continued, 'my cousin in the Indian Civil telling me of just such an escape tunnel being constructed at the theatre at Simla, the Indian summer capital. It was used to evacuate the Viceroy from the royal box during a sectarian riot, sometime in the eighties, I believe.'

Shaw tapped and pushed at various panels for some time, and then turned to Palgrave.

'There is perhaps some secret mechanism to open the panelling, if we could but find it…'

After a fruitless search of several minutes, Palgrave placed a hand on Shaw's shoulder.

'If such a passage did exist,' he said, somewhat in the manner of somebody talking to a disappointed child, 'it would surely be known about by the Clerk of Works, the chap who looks after the fabric of the building. There will be something about it in the archives. Why don't we have a look there?'

'Very well,' sighed Shaw. 'Perhaps I was expecting too much, too soon.'

'Come along,' replied Palgrave. 'I'm taking the Lower Fourth for prep soon, and you'll need to get back to your conference.'

'Of course,' said Shaw. 'Might we examine the archives this evening?'

'Don't see why not,' said Palgrave. 'The Clerk of Works isn't there often, but I don't think it's ever locked. We could go tonight. I'm giving an organ recital but should be finished by eight.'

'Very well,' said Shaw. 'Until tonight then. Shall we go down?'

The two men moved towards the staircase. Shaw stopped, and peered intently at the floorboards by the row of pews facing the balcony's edge. He bent down, and picked up a small scrap of paper which had been partially obscured by the base of the pew.

'Hello,' said Palgrave. 'Found a clue?'

'Possibly,' said Shaw, as he held the scrap up to the light. 'it has writing on it.'

'What does it say?'

'It does not make sense. Here.'

Shaw handed the scrap to Palgrave. It had on it four lines of writing, with only one word on each line, which Palgrave read out loud.

'"ny, le, sin, O, tree."' What on earth does it mean? Is it French? Some sort of religious reference?'

'"Le sin" does not sound right to me,' said Shaw. 'I think their word is *péché*. Your French is probably better than mine however.'

'Perhaps. I'm certainly likely to have had more experience of sin in France than you.' Palgrave grinned boyishly.

'The less said about that the better,' said Shaw.

'If it's not French, then what is it?' asked Palgrave. 'And "ny" – New York, perhaps? But that's usually written in capitals. What could it mean?'

''I have no idea,' replied Shaw. 'It could perhaps be part

of a longer sentence. At any rate, I ought to show it to the police. They must have missed it when they searched here.'

'Very well,' said Palgrave. He looked at his wristwatch. 'Look here, I must dash. The Lower Fourth are apt to wreak havoc if left alone too long.'

'Of course,' said Shaw, who put the scrap of paper carefully away in his wallet.

When the two men reached the foot of the spiral staircase, they were met by Pettigrew.

'I say,' said Palgrave to the verger. 'Any idea why that chair's in the corner up there?'

'That chair sir?' asked Pettigrew. 'I've no idea. It's been there as long as I've been going up to put out the Dean's prayer-book. Furniture's not my pigeon. Why?'

Palgrave was about to speak again, but was interrupted by the stern official voice of Inspector Wragg.

'I turn my back five minutes in this place and already my instructions have been countermanded. What were these men doing up there? I saw them coming down the stairs.'

'I'm sorry, Inspector,' said Pettigrew. 'I didn't realise that you were coming…'

'Oh, so you were the "look-out"', eh?' said Wragg. 'Posted there to give a whistle if the police turned up, I suppose. You can go.'

Mumbling further apologies, Pettigrew scuttled quickly away.

'I'd like a word with you two gents though, if you don't mind,' added the Inspector.

'We are both in rather a hurry,' said Palgrave. 'Can it wait?'

'No it cannot,' said Wragg. 'I made it quite clear nobody was to go up on that balcony but it looks as if you two

110

have decided to ignore that.'

'I'm not sure I like your tone, Inspector,' said Palgrave, bristling. 'I'm fairly certain you don't have any authority to bar cathedral staff, and their guests, from going about their lawful occasions on the premises. So would you kindly state your business?'

Shaw could not help but smile at Palgrave's withering reply, speaking to the Inspector as if he were a miscreant private on a charge. The Inspector seemed slightly taken aback, and moderated his manner slightly.

'Well, I…that is, it's dangerous up there, so we don't want anybody poking around. What were you doing up there anyway?'

'That is none of your concern,' said Palgrave.

'It's all right, Inspector,' said Shaw. 'We were testing a theory. You see, both of us believe it unlikely that Mr Vale could have fallen off the balcony by accident.'

Wragg bridled. 'I've told you already, Mr Shaw, I don't take kindly to amateurs poking their nose into things that don't concern them. Now I don't want to have to tell you again.'

'Now look here…' began Palgrave angrily, but Shaw cut him off.

'Of course, Inspector. Then you will not wish to see a small clue that we have found.'

Shaw's attempt to interest the Inspector fell on deaf ears. 'No I do not,' said the policeman. 'My men have already checked that gallery and if there was anything worth finding they would have told me. As we have already stated, the fall was an accident. If it was anything more, that is for the coroner to decide, but for the moment I would be grateful if you two gentlemen would go about your own business and allow me to go about mine. I shall speak to the new Dean to ensure my wishes are carried out.

Good day.'

'Oh, one more thing, Inspector,' said Shaw.

'Yes?' asked Wragg, without attempting to disguise his annoyance.

'Are you familiar with the name Cyril Peach?'

Wragg's face curled in disgust.

'What the devil…of course I am, I arrested him outside this very cathedral. What are you asking about that filthy blighter for?'

'Is it possible he may be wandering about in the cathedral precincts again?' asked Shaw tentatively.

Wragg let out a bitter laugh. 'My word, you really do take this amateur detection thing seriously, don't you?'

'It was a perfectly civil question,' said Shaw firmly.

'All right,' replied Wragg slowly, 'Then I'll give you a civil answer, but for the last time, mark you. Cyril Peach is never going to be wandering about anywhere again, unless he's in an invalid-chair. He fell down some stairs in prison – his sort sometimes do – and he lost the use of his legs, permanently. Rough justice, if you ask me. Now, if you'll excuse me, I have my job to get on with and I expect you have yours.'

The Inspector strode off towards the west door, and Palgrave blew out his cheeks.

'Well, of all the blasted…who does he think he is?'

'He perhaps has a point,' said Shaw. 'We really do not have any business interfering. I must go.'

'And I,' added Palgrave. 'But we'll still have a look in the archives tonight, eh? And perhaps we'll find your secret passage. Cheerio.'

Shaw was deep in thought as he walked through the cathedral cloisters towards Diocesan House. Perhaps the Inspector was right, and he ought not to get involved. He had already made one wrong assumption based on very thin evidence. But if it was not Cyril Peach he had seen loitering in the cathedral grounds at night, then who was it?

Skinner heard a faint knock on his bedroom door but ignored it; his head throbbed from the whisky he had consumed and he wanted nothing more than to sleep the whole day through. The knock came again and a soft voice called his name.

'Lennie…Lennie love, are you awake? I've brought you a cup of tea.'

God, he thought. It was *her*. He knew this would happen. Get too close to a woman and she starts thinking there's something going on between you and her, even women like Queenie who should know better.

'Don't want any,' mumbled Skinner, but Queenie did not seem to hear him. She bustled into the room and put a cup and saucer on the bedside table.

'There you are,' she said with a smile. 'That'll pick you up. I wondered where you'd got to. Taking an afternoon nap at your age! You sure you're not sickening for something?'

Sickening to get you off my back, thought Skinner, who struggled into a sitting position.

'Turn your back will you, while I get my trousers on,' he said.

'No need to be coy.'

'I said turn your bleeding back!'

'Charmed I'm sure!'

Queenie pouted, and turned to face the dust-laden dresser by the bed. She began examining and re-arranging

Skinner's personal effects, including the little slips of paper on which he wrote down his customers' bets.

'You need a woman's touch in here,' she said. 'This room depresses me.'

So do you, Skinner was about to say as he pulled his trouser braces over his shoulders, but instead he buttoned up his flies and took a sip of tea. It tasted good; hot and sweet the way he liked it. Would it be so bad, after all, to have a regular woman around, and…he took a deep breath. Skinny, my boy, he said to himself, you are getting weak.

He lit a cigarette and squinted through the smoke at Queenie.

'What do you want? I've got stuff to do.'

He looked across at the betting slips re-arranged by Queenie, and thrust his hand in his trouser pocket to check if any more were there. He suddenly felt something that was very close to fear, although he had never really understood what such a thing was.

'I'm worried about you,' said Queenie. 'You haven't been yourself since that to-do yesterday. What was it all about? Why didn't we do what we arranged?'

'Never mind all that,' said Skinner. 'Change of plan.'

He had to think. How much did she know? And was she a risk? She can't have seen the papers, he thought, or she would be asking questions. The papers! His eyes darted to that morning's *East Anglian Daily Times*, where he had left it on the chair beside the bed.

'Oh, is that today's?' asked Queenie, following Skinner's gaze to the newspaper. 'I must have a look. There's this new thing in there called a "horoscope". They invented it for Princess Margaret, would you believe it? It tells you all about your future. Like tea leaves, only more accurate. Elsie down at the Rose and Crown says hers told her she would get married and do you know, three months later she did? Chance would be a fine thing for me, of course, but you never know, and…'

'I haven't read it yet, leave it be,' said Skinner, who made a grab for the paper.

'Oh, be a sport,' said Queenie playfully, and snatched the paper up before he could grasp it. She slapped the paper down on the bed and, once on her knees on the threadbare carpet, began smoothing out the front page.

'I said leave that blasted…' Skinner did not finish his sentence. It was too late – he could tell from Queenie's face what she had seen.

'Here…' she whispered. 'Dean of Midchester Cathedral dies in fall from…but that was where you…'

She stood up as Skinner's shadow obscured the paper. He was standing close to her, but it was not the closeness of an embrace.

'I'm sorry Queenie,' he whispered. 'I didn't want it to be this way.' She suddenly felt her blood run cold as Skinner's hands encircled her neck.

Dusk was setting in as Shaw made his way back from Diocesan House to the Cathedral Close. The afternoon lecture had been extremely dry, delivered by a clergyman with a monotonous, soporific voice. Shaw had felt his thoughts constantly drifting away to the matter of Vale's death.

Was he, he wondered, becoming too involved? The Inspector had already warned him away from amateur detection, and his tentative theory about Cyril Peach had been exposed as hopelessly ill-informed. Perhaps, he thought, he had better just forget about the incident and concentrate on delivering his remaining lectures, and then return home.

As he crossed Cathedral Green, he suddenly noticed a figure walking across the south side of the cathedral. A figure in a beige raincoat and cap. Without losing a moment, he followed, making sure he was not seen. The figure rounded the cathedral to the west wall, but when Shaw cautiously looked round it, idling in the manner of one looking at gravestones, the individual had completely disappeared.

After a few minutes of dawdling, Shaw decided whoever it was, was not coming back. He might, after all, simply be one of many men who wore a cap and a raincoat. He began to wander back to the Cathedral Close, deep in thought.

He let himself into Palgrave's house with the latch-key he had been loaned, and saw on the table the cold supper left by Mrs Snelgrove. He was tempted to begin eating, but decided it was too early and that he ought to wait for Palgrave. It was chilly and damp in the room, and there was no fire in the grate. Staring at the gathering gloom through the window, Shaw suddenly felt very much alone. He must, he thought, write to his wife.

He climbed the steep staircase and rummaged in his bag for paper and pen, then stopped. He fumbled in his trouser pocket and checked his change; he had several pennies and decided it would not be overly extravagant to telephone instead; he longed to hear Marion's voice and all the inconsequential news of the village.

There was a telephone box, he recalled, at the far end of the Close. He took his coat from the hook on the back of the door and put it on. He then switched off the electric light. Suddenly in the darkness he was able to see clearly through the bedroom window, and there, again, was a figure, standing by the back gate on the river path, his face just visible in the reddish glow from a cigarette.

Unlike the previous figure with his fawn coloured raincoat and cap, this man had on a dark overcoat and trilby hat. He was clearly watching the house, and for a moment, Shaw fancied their eyes met, although he could not make them out at such a distance.

Without further thought, Shaw bounded downstairs and out into the Cathedral Close. He walked briskly through the little side passageway which led from the Close to the river path. When he emerged on to the path, he slowed his pace slightly to appear as if he were just out for a stroll.

The man must have noticed him, for he began walking away quickly. Shaw increased his speed, and the man did likewise; he dodged into the next passageway, through which Shaw pursued him. The passageway led back out to the Cathedral Close where it joined the Green, but when Shaw emerged, the man seemed to have disappeared.

Shaw looked round in bewilderment, but before he knew what was happening, two men walked briskly alongside him and he felt himself gripped firmly by each arm and almost bodily lifted as they continued to walk along, like two boozers helping home a drunken companion.

'Don't call out, don't look round, and get in,' ordered the larger of the two men quietly, albeit in a tone which suggested Shaw ought not to argue with him. There was the roar of a powerful engine and a screech of brakes, as a large, dark motor car pulled up beside them on the cobbled street.

Before he really knew what was happening, he felt a hand push his head down, and he was bundled into the back seat of the vehicle. Doors slammed and then his body jerked backwards as the car drove rapidly away.

Millicent looked out cautiously from the the copse between the cathedral grounds and the river, where she had fled back to after she had seen the man coming her way. There had been something familiar about him, but he was too far away to recognise.

What was certain, she thought, was that he was following her. She could not possibly risk trying to enter the cathedral again until it was fully dark, so she decided to wait. She simply must get what she had come for – there was no alternative. But she also could not risk being seen.

As the dusk deepened, she saw more men; two of them, walking around the cathedral grounds, as if searching for something – or some*one*. Then, a large, black, official looking motor-car had sped past her on the gravel path, inches away from where she was hiding. She closed her eyes, with some atavistic childish hope that such an action would prevent her from being seen. Perhaps it worked, because the car continued on its way, leaving only the sound of the dusk twitterings of birds.

She decided to risk it; if she waited any longer, the servants might start wondering where she was, seeing as she had been out all day without telling them when she would be back. She was pretty sure the gates of the cathedral grounds would be locked soon as well, and she could not risk being seen climbing over them, which would mark her out as a definite intruder. She walked briskly across the gravel path and through the open gates which led into the grounds.

A distance of some twenty yards lay between her and the north transept of the cathedral. Her heart pounding, she took a deep breath and walked at a slow but steady pace, with her hands behind her back, pausing momentarily to pretend she was examining some of the graves.

She stopped at the north wall of the cathedral, by a huge flying buttress. Night had now almost completely enveloped the cathedral, and the only illumination was that of dimmed lamps shining through the stained glass windows. She realised she had never been here in the dark before. She felt in the pocket of her raincoat, but she had forgotten to bring cigarettes and matches. The light, she decided, might attract too much attention anyway.

She began to panic. Where on earth was it – the place she was looking for? It had seemed so obvious during the day, when she had last been there, that she was amazed that nobody else knew about it. But now, all seemed gloom and shadows, the grass far more overgrown and sodden than she remembered. She must *think!*

Suddenly she heard voices from the direction of the south door, and the noise of footsteps on the gravel path. It could not be a service, as she knew that Evensong would be finished by now; then she remembered. Tom's organ recital! He had mentioned it at luncheon the day before. There must be people going in. If she stood still, there was no reason for them to notice her on this side of the cathedral. She then flinched as the light of a battery torch played upon her.

'Hi, you there!' came a stern voice.

She raised a hand in front of her face, partly to shield her eyes from the glare, and partly to prevent anyone seeing her face. She made out the shape of an old fashioned top hat and cape on the silhouetted figure ahead of her. It must be one of the beadles, she realised; the cathedral night-watchmen who wore an obsolete uniform on special occasions such as a public concert.

'These precincts is out of bounds after dark,' came the voice again. 'I'm locking the gates so be on your way.'

Millicent was about to apologise, in that way that well-bred English people sometimes do too readily to figures of authority, but checked herself. She *must* not be recognised. It was hopeless to remain here any longer.

The man began walking toward her. She turned and fled, and within moments returned to where she had hidden Bounder in the copse. As she mounted him she chanced to look up, and in the dim light of a passing motorcar's headlamps, she noticed an object wedged in the branches above her head. She reached for it, and almost cried with relief, shoving it in her raincoat pocket firmly lest it disappear like some apparition.

She shook Bounder's reins briskly and rode off in the direction of Mead Lodge as quickly as she dared.

Chapter Eight

Shaw's first instinct on being thrust into the motor car was to struggle, but in the confined space at the rear of the vehicle, and with his arms still pinioned by his sides, such a reaction was impossible.

'You can slow down a bit now, Phillips,' said the taller of the two men to the driver. 'I don't think we'll be seen from here on in. Head for the main west road, will you?'

'Right you are sir,' said the driver, without turning his head. The car began to slow down as it encountered a traffic block on the main road which lead out of Midchester. Shaw momentarily considered escape, now that the car was going at walking pace, but before he could work out how to execute such a plan, the taller man released his grip, and addressed him in a friendly manner.

'I'm sorry about all the cloak-and-dagger stuff, Mr Shaw,' he said. 'Only we're not too sure who's about that Cathedral Close at the moment. Perhaps you don't remember me?'

Shaw looked at the man's face, with its slim, slightly aristocratic features, then suddenly realised who he was.

'Superintendent Gregory! Of Special Branch.'

'Well remembered sir. It was a few years ago now.'

'Indeed. Almost four years. I could hardly forget, however. The assassination of King Basil* will haunt me to

*See The King is Dead.

the end of my days.'

'Yes, it was a nasty business,' replied Gregory. 'But we got the killer in the end, thanks mainly of course to you.'

Gregory gestured to the man on Shaw's other side. 'Oh, by the way, this gentleman is Major Wheatley.'

Shaw turned to face the man. He had thick-set, jowly features, a drinker's nose, and a brush of a moustache.

'How do,' said the man brusquely, keeping his gaze straight ahead.

'Major Wheatley works for…' began Gregory, but he was cut off.

'For a certain department of His Majesty's Government, Mr Shaw,' said Wheatley, in an accent which suggested he had not been born into the social class which generally produces officers of his rank. 'Let's leave it at that, shall we?'

The car was now on the new Midchester bypass road, and began to pick up speed as the traffic thinned out.

'I don't understand what all this is about,' said Shaw. 'Has there been some development in the case concerning King Basil's death? I was led to believe that was all over.'

'In a way, there is something of a vague connection,' said Gregory. 'But first of all, I really must apologise again about man-handling you into the car. I promise I shall make it all clear presently. Have you had dinner?'

'I have not eaten since lunch time,' said Shaw, who suddenly felt very hungry indeed.

'Good,' said Gregory with a smile. 'Then let's have something.'

'That sounds excellent,' said Shaw. 'But I must get word to Palgrave, that is, the gentleman with whom I…'

'We know who he is, Mr Shaw,' said Gregory crisply, 'and don't worry, a message will be sent to him.'

'Very well,' said Shaw.

'There's a quiet little place not far from here,' continued the Superintendent, 'where we can have a little chat. They do a good meat and two veg., and keep an excellent claret. If that's all right with you, Major Wheatley?'

'Couldn't care less about what filthy French plonk they dish up, as long as there's good ale on tap,' replied the Major.

'Very well,' said Gregory, with what Shaw thought was the faintest hint of irritation in his voice. 'Phillips,' he said to the driver, 'take the Norwich Road, to just before Elmsworth. And put your foot down or we'll miss the best cuts off the joint.'

Skinner edged his way cautiously along the King's Gallery, keeping to the wall where he knew he could not be seen. It was annoying, he thought, that there were still people in the cathedral – there seemed to be some sort of service or musical concert going on – but the advantage of this was that low lights were on in the building, sufficient for him to see what he was doing. In pitch darkness, he would have needed to use a battery torch, and that might have attracted attention from outside.

The gloomy sound of the organ drifted up to the balcony; Skinner shivered. He disliked churches. As a child his mother had sometimes dumped him in a Sunday School held in a tin chapel when she was entertaining a gentleman friend and wanted him out of the house.

Back then, he saw the institution of the church as no different to that of the school he was forced to attend during the week; something contrived purely to force him to sit still, keep quiet and do anything other than that which he wanted to do, except that the Sunday School was run by effete do-gooders instead of the petty tyrants at his elementary school. Having not attended a church again since the age of eleven, his views had had no opportunity to change.

He disliked church music as well; organs were all right in picture palaces, he thought, if they played a jolly tune, but the dirges they pumped out in churches just made a man feel like he needed a drink.

He licked his lips. He could do with a drink now, he thought, but had forgotten his flask; and besides, there was work to do. He got down on his hands and knees. Anyone looking up from down below could not possibly see him. He scoured the floor as quietly as he could, feeling around under the row of pews and running his thumb along the edge of floorboards; nothing. Had the police already found what he was looking for, and established a connection?

Unlikely, he thought. If they had, they would have been sure to have come looking for him by now. Was it, instead, somewhere so out of sight that even the 'tecs hadn't found it? Perhaps. Perhaps it wasn't even here at all, and he should just stop worrying. With the Dean dead and Queenie gone as well, there was very little to worry about now anyway. Best to go home and forget all about it. He smiled, and crawled backwards into the shadows.

'Not a bad little place, Gregory, not a bad little place at all', said Major Wheatley, as he stifled a belch. 'Very suitable, I shouldn't wonder, for a chap wanting to have a discreet little week-end away from the wife with a...' He paused, seeming to remember he was in the presence of a man of the cloth, and then continued. 'Anyway, I suppose you gents will be having cigars now,' he continued as he pushed his plate away. 'I'll make do with a fag myself.'

'Thank you, but my pipe is sufficient for me,' said Shaw. 'I do not wish to take advantage of your hospitality any further. The meal was excellent, but if you could kindly tell me what you want of me, I shall find my way back to Midchester.'

'Don't thank me,' said Wheatley. 'Thank the British taxpayer. It's him that's paying for it.'

The three men were seated in a curtained alcove of a small hotel and restaurant in the west of Suffolk known as The Bream, a place where peacocks haunted the topiary and a gurgling brook ran close by, with a little arched bridge on which guests could have their photograph taken for one shilling and sixpence.

Gregory and Wheatley had told Shaw they would make everything clear to him, but that he ought to enjoy his dinner first before they got down to business. He could not help wondering whether this was some sort of delaying tactic designed to test him in some way, but then he decided he was letting his imagination get the better of him again.

Gregory took a cigar proffered by a silent waiter, cut the end off it with a small knife, and puffed contentedly for a few moments before speaking.

'We've had Midchester Cathedral in our sights for some time,' said the Superintendent, who took the cigar out of his mouth and looked reflectively at its glowing end. 'Do you know, Mr Shaw, what a P.O.I is?'

'A police, something or other?' assayed the clergyman. He disliked acronyms, and wished people would not use them, but it seemed to be another aspect of the modern world against which it was almost hopeless to fight.

'A Person of Interest,' replied Gregory. 'Not exactly a suspect in the legal sense, but someone we keep an eye on.'

'And there is such at person at the cathedral?' asked Shaw.

'Was,' said Wheatley bluntly, as he stubbed out his cigarette and lit another. 'Reverend Eckhart Vale.'

'The late Dean?' exclaimed Shaw. 'What on earth for?'

'Come along, Mr Shaw,' said Gregory. 'He was well known as a communist sympathiser. He didn't even try to hide it. That business with the red flag up in the church, for example.'

'An ill-advised act for a clergyman, I agree,' said Shaw, 'but I fail to see why it is a matter in which the police should take an interest. He had committed no crime.'

Wheatley sighed, and drained the last of the brandy from his glass. He grimaced with distaste, and snapped his fingers loudly until the silent waiter put his head around the tapestry curtain.

'Here, sonny, get me a pint of bitter, will you? I need to rinse my mouth out after this French muck.'

Shaw noticed the faintest raising of Gregory's left eyebrow; the waiter's face however betrayed no hint of emotion and he withdrew as silently as he had arrived.

'Look, Mr Shaw,' continued Wheatley. 'I'm a straight talking man, and perhaps it's best if I take over from Superintendent Gregory at this point. I only asked him along because I knew you'd met him on the King Basil affair and I thought a friendly face might help things along. But it's me that's running this show, see?'

'You mean it is not a police matter?' asked Shaw.

'I work with Superintendent Gregory and Special Branch, yes,' said Wheatley, 'but I'm not a policeman.'

'The army, then?' enquired Shaw with some confusion in his voice. He frowned as he began to fill his pipe.

'As I said before,' replied Wheatley, 'don't worry too much about who I'm working for. Think of me as a sort of civil servant, only one who carries a revolver instead of an umbrella.'

He laughed uproariously at his own attempt at humour, then looked up as the silent waiter placed a pint of foaming beer next to him.

'Thanks sonny,' he said. 'I need to talk and my mouth's as dry as an arab's sandal. Run along now.'

This time the waiter did lift one of his eyebrows an infinitesimal amount, and he disappeared quickly behind the curtain.

'Ah, that's better,' said Wheatley, after he had drunk almost half the pint of beer in one swallow. 'Now, where was I. Ah yes. The late Dean of Midchester. He was a blasted Red, and we've had orders to keep an eye on his sort in positions of public responsibility.'

'Including the church?' asked Shaw.

'Particularly including the church,' said Wheatley. 'All the institutions have got them now, this is how they work, they hollow out places from the inside. Happening over in America too. Perhaps not your actual Reds, but Pinks at least. Sympathisers. Give 'em free rein, and the whole lot collapses and before you know it we're another colony of Mother Russia.'

'Do you mean to say the Dean was some sort of Russian spy?' said Shaw.

'Well...' said Wheatley doubtfully, 'not as such. But we had to keep an eye on him just the same. So when he got bumped, er, I mean, had his tragic accident, I was notified by my department, and little bells started ringing.'

'Little bells?' asked Shaw, as he lit his pipe.

'Yes,' said Wheatley. 'In my head. I thought to myself, communist agents in Suffolk? Now where have I heard that before? Ah yes, says I, last time I heard of anything like that was with Superintendent Gregory's lot over in Lower Tuddenham.'

'Lower Addenham,' corrected Gregory.

'Could be lower intestine for all I care,' said Wheatley disdainfully. 'Anyway, I thought, better have a look, so I motored down here, on the QT, and made a few discreet enquiries round the cathedral.

'The first thing I looked at was the list of people attending that conference, as there were a lot of intellectual types and any one of them might be wrong 'uns. And one name on that list set another little bell ringing. Reverend Shaw, of All Saint's Church, Lower Addenham. I've got the name right this time, haven't I?' Wheatley smiled a nicotine-stained smile at the other two men.

Shaw swallowed. 'Do you mean to imply I am some sort of suspect?'

'Nothing of the kind, Mr Shaw,' said Gregory with a smile. 'Rather, we think you may be able to help us.'

'I'll speak plainly again,' said Wheatley. 'We think it's possible Vale's death wasn't an accident. We need to find out if he was bumped off by the Reds.'

'You really think he was killed by some sort of…Russian agents?' asked Shaw. 'A few years ago I would have said that was fantastical, but then again, after the assassination of King Basil…'

'Exactly,' said Gregory. 'The Soviets have agents operating in England. We know that for a fact. And it's possible that the Dean somehow got on the wrong side of them, and they decided to get rid of him. It's the sort of thing they've been doing all over Europe in recent years.'

'Only now,' said Wheatley, 'to make matters worse, we've got the blasted Germans to watch as well.'

'Germans?' asked Shaw. 'What have they to do with it?'

'Until last year we only had the Russians to worry about,' said Wheatley. 'But now, since Herr Hitler's been elected, we think he's got people working in this country as well. And nobody hates the Reds more than his National Socialist Party, despite the name. It could be that Vale fell foul of one of *his* lot. We just don't know.'

'But this is preposterous,' said Shaw. 'After all, the newspapers tell us that Herr Hitler is a buffer to the approach of communism. Surely he would not send agents to kill English clergymen?'

'You ought not to believe all you read in the papers,' said Wheatley. 'If you know what my department knows, you'll know that Herr Hitler's lot aren't much different to the Bolshies and perhaps even worse. He's a friend of England at the moment, supposedly, but we'll have trouble with him, you mark my words.'

'At present we're keeping an open mind,' said Gregory. 'We're not opening a formal investigation. We haven't the grounds, nor the manpower, if it comes to that.'

He looked down at his cigar again, and gently tapped the heavy ash from its tip into the ashtray before him. 'And that, Mr Shaw,' he continued, 'is where *you* come in.'

'More sherry, Chancel...I mean, Mr Dean?' asked Mrs Vale as she proffered the newly opened bottle to Adams, who sat opposite her in the drawing room.

'Ah...a small glass, please, Mrs Vale,' he said. 'It is excellent quality, so I do not wish to exploit your hospitality.'

'No matter,' said Mrs Vale, as she topped up his glass to the brim. 'I have decided that, if I am to eke out the remainder of my days in genteel poverty, I may as well enjoy myself while I am still able. Oh, and please do not be concerned. This bottle came from my husband's private supply. It was not taken from the cellars here, which you will of course be in charge of once you move in as Dean. Your very good health.'

She raised her equally brimming glass and took a large gulp of the golden liquid. 'You'll stay to dinner, of course?'

Adams felt uncomfortable alone in the house of the recently deceased Dean. He could not help feeling that the widow, despite her weeds, did not seem to be quite as grief-stricken as one might expect. She seemed, if he was honest with himself, almost light-hearted about it all, despite her protestations of impending poverty.

'Ah, I think not, thank you all the same,' he said, taking another sip of sherry. 'I have so much work to do. The er, the funeral arrangements, and so on…'

'Of course,' said Mrs Vale with a smile. 'I myself have dozens of letters to write, and all sorts of legal formalities to conduct, but do you know, Dr Adams...oh, sorry, I mean, Mr Dean. Or is Dr Dean?'

'Dr Adams will do,' said Adams. 'The more formal title is for Chapter members.'

'Very well,' replied Mrs Vale. 'Dr Adams, do you know, I really am not much in the mood for playing the grieving widow this evening.'

She sat back against the sofa cushions, her slim black form stark against the light Regency stripe pattern of the upholstery, and smiled mysteriously at him.

Adams swallowed. Was the woman flirting with him? He really did not know if she was; he was the sort of man who had never had much time for women, nor they for him. 'Piggy' had been his nickname at school, and he knew that he had a face that bore a passing resemblance to that particular animal. He suddenly wondered if she had designs on him in order to keep the house which would soon be occupied by him; he then mentally chastised himself for such an uncharitable thought.

'We all need to take our mind off things for a while,' said Adams, feeling more comfortable as he slipped into preaching mode. 'Reading the scriptures, I find, is most...'

'I'm not particularly interested in the scriptures at present,' replied Mrs Vale suddenly, with a smile. 'Does that shock you?'

'We all of us go through periods of spiritual, ah, weakness,' replied Adams. 'I suggest you pray about it, and...'

'You misunderstand me, Dr Adams,' said Mrs Vale. 'I did not ask you here for spiritual advice. The Lord knows I received enough of that from my late husband. I wanted to know what you know about a certain Reverend Lucian Shaw.'

'Shaw?' asked Adams with slight confusion. 'You mean the man here for the conference?'

'That is correct.'

'I have met him briefly. What about him?'

'I have previously read accounts of him in the newspapers, which claim he is some sort of amateur detective. Is that right?'

'Well, er...he has assisted the police in a number of investigations, I believe.'

'Very well. Would you be so kind as to introduce us?'

'What for?'

'Dr Adams,' replied Mrs Vale as she poured herself another glass of sherry, 'up until this week I was of the naive opinion that the British police were the best in the world.'

Adams noticed she had not offered him another drink;

131

he decided he had better sip his slowly as he might need his wits about him.

'You are unhappy about their response to your husband's death?' he asked.

'To a certain extent. If the representatives of the Suffolk Constabulary I spoke to are the best in the world, then I dread to think what the police are like in less happy lands.'

'Do you...ah...have suspicions that your husband's death was...'

'Was not an accident?' prompted Mrs Vale. 'perhaps, but what concerns me more is the the police seem singularly uninterested in discussing it. I thought perhaps Mr Shaw might have some theories of his own.'

Adams suddenly felt uncomfortably hot; there was a large fire blazing in the hearth. In his own house he never indulged in such luxury until the first Sunday in Advent.

'Do you, ah, have any evidence that your husband's death was *not* an accident?' asked Adams warily. 'Any particular persons that you think could have had reason to...'

'Perhaps,' said Mrs Vale.

'May I know whom?'

'Not at present. I would prefer to speak to Mr Shaw about it rather than advertise my theories to all and sundry.'

Adams bridled at such a description, and replied somewhat coldly.

'I think it would be best to allow the police, and His Majesty's Coroner, to do their jobs, Mrs Vale,' he said after a pause. 'From what Inspector Wragg has said to me, it seems our Mr Shaw may be something of a, well, a meddler. Causing more trouble than he is worth, so to say.'

'Very well, Dr Adams, I take your point,' said Mrs Vale,

who downed the last of her sherry decisively. 'I realise I cannot compel you to introduce us, so I shall leave a card with him presently. Thank you so much for coming – do not let me keep you.'

Adams sensed a new authority in Mrs Vale, who hitherto seemed to have been a lesser adjunct to her husband. He had the distinct impression he had been dismissed, and so took his leave without finishing the rest of his sherry.

'I still don't understand what it is you want me to do,' said Shaw. 'Inspector Wragg made it quite clear that I was not to get involved in any enquiries concerning the Dean's death.'

He sat in the rear of the large black motor-car again with Wheatley beside him, but this time Gregory sat in the front passenger seat. The vehicle sped along empty roads through the black night towards Midchester, passing oil-lit cottages and shuttered villages in which the occasional glare of an electric street lamp momentarily illuminated the faces of the car's occupants.

'Don't worry yourself about what that hayseed says,' said Wheatley, with a half-stifled belch. 'We've had words with fellows a bit further up his chain of command. A *lot* further up. He won't stand in your way, we'll see to that.'

'But…' objected Shaw.

'All we're asking,' said Gregory, half-turning towards the rear of the car, 'is that you keep your ear to the ground, as it were. Do a bit of asking around. But for heaven's sake keep it discreet.'

'Do you mean to say you wish me to be some sort of

police informer?' asked Shaw, with a note of distaste in his voice.

'Nothing of the sort,' said Gregory smoothly. 'Just go about your normal business at the conference over the next few days but see what you can find out in the meantime. Anything that might indicate Vale's death was deliberate. Think of yourself as just doing your public duty, only in perhaps a slightly more formal way than the average citizen. We'll reimburse any expense incurred.'

'But ought not such investigations be carried out by trained men, such as those of your, ah, organisation?' asked Shaw.

'As I mentioned earlier, Mr Shaw,' said Gregory, 'we can't justify putting anyone on this case until we definitely know something suspicious is going on. If there *are* Reds involved...'

'Or Huns,' interjected Wheatley with a hiccup.

'Or...Germans,' continued Gregory, 'we can't trust Wragg's lot with it. They're not suitable for an enquiry of that delicacy and if they know there's something like that going on they'll likely make a hash of it. One of them will talk about it in a public house and it will be all over the town before we know it.'

'But then why trust me?' said Shaw. 'I am just an ordinary clergyman.'

'That's the beauty of it,' said Wheatley. 'No Red agent, if there *is* one, is going to notice some parson asking questions here and there around a cathedral. It's what we call "undercover" work in our business. But we don't have any men who could pass themselves off as holy, believe you me. Most of them are godless ba...'

'I see,' interrupted Shaw. 'Very well. I shall make some enquiries. But that is all. I am a minister of religion, not a detective, and I am certainly not some sort of

134

"undercover" operative.'

'That's just the attitude we want, Mr Shaw,' said Wheatley genially. 'And let us know anything you find out. There's a telephone number here. Someone will answer it, at any time of the day or night.'

He passed a business card to Shaw, who squinted at it, and read it out loud. "Universal Imports, 12 Fleming Place, London W2. Telephone Regent 3914." I don't understand.'

'You don't think we give out cards saying who we really are?,' asked Wheatley with a chuckle.

Shaw felt his face flush. 'Of course,' he said sheepishly, and put the card in his pocket.

'Don't do that Mr Shaw,' continued Wheatley. 'You've got to memorise that number and then swallow that card.'

Shaw reached back into his pocket but was stopped by Wheatley who grabbed his arm with his fat fingers, laughing loudly. Shaw noticed with distaste the man was drunker than he had first appeared.

'Oh that's priceless,' he said between gasps. 'You should have seen his face, Gregory! He would have done it, too! Cheer up Mr Shaw, it's only my fun!'

A flicker of irritation passed over Gregory's otherwise impassive features as he looked round, then turned back to face the driver as the car slowed down on the approach to Midchester's city centre.

'Stop over there by that cinema, Phillips,' he ordered. 'We won't get noticed in the traffic block. Sorry Mr Shaw, we'd better not risk leaving you at the Cathedral Close, but it's only a ten minute walk from here. Now remember, *be discreet*. Keep it to yourself, eh? I don't want to be theatrical, but I ought to remind you, you are bound by the Official Secrets Act.'

Shaw got out of the car but then his arm was stayed by Wheatley's podgy hand. 'I was joking about the card Mr

Shaw, but I'm not joking when I say this. If you ever have to telephone, don't use my name. You won't get anywhere. Ask for Mr Sands instead.'

'Who is he?' asked Shaw.

'Nobody,' replied Wheatley. 'Sort of a code name. But you'll get put through to me or one of my lot. Got it?'

'Yes, I think so,' said Shaw doubtfully, wondering if it were another joke; Wheatley's impassive features suggested it was not.

'Good night then, Mr Shaw,' said Wheatley, and pulled the door shut.

A few moments later Shaw had mingled with the crowd pouring out of the cinema, and he began walking towards the black spire of the cathedral which towered over the squares and lanes of the medieval city.

His last view of the car as it sped away showed him Wheatley laughing uproariously to himself on the back seat as Gregory and the driver stared ahead into the night.

Chapter Nine

When Shaw arrived at the Cathedral Close, he made a brief telephone call from the public kiosk, assuring his wife that all was well (not perhaps the whole truth, he thought, but he did not wish to worry her). He then let himself into Palgrave's house with his borrowed latchkey, to find his old friend finishing off the supper left for them by Mrs Snelgrove.

'Where on earth did you get to?' he asked. 'I was beginning to think you'd been done in by the ghostly cathedral assassin.'

Shaw smiled weakly. 'I...bumped into an old acquaintance. Or rather, he bumped into me. I understood he sent word.'

'Ah, that explains it then,' replied Palgrave. 'The porter knocked on the door with a telephone message saying you wouldn't be back until late, but it didn't say where you'd gone.'

Shaw could not help admiring the efficiency of Superintendent Gregory, but he now realised he would have to be careful in what he said to his friend.

'Never mind, old chap,' said Palgave between mouthfuls. I'm afraid I've eaten all our rations. I assume, as the Scotsman said, "you'll have had your dinner"?'

'Ah...yes,' replied Shaw. 'How was the organ recital?'

'Oh, nothing special,' replied Palgrave. 'It's supposed to

raise funds for the cathedral but I can't think we got more than tuppence ha'penny in the plate. Here's an odd thing though. I spoke to Harris, one of the beadles, while he was locking up, and he said our suspicious character was lurking in the grounds again.'

'Suspicious character?' asked Shaw guardedly.

'Yes. Slim, fair hair. Wearing a fawn raincoat. Hanging about by the east window. Harris challenged him and he dashed off.'

'A cause for concern, do you think?'

'Perhaps not,' said Palgrave. 'Probably just a drunk looking for a convenient wall on his way home. People have no respect these days.'

'Indeed,' said Shaw. He looked at his watch. It was nearly half past nine. 'My dear fellow, I must apologise. I recall we were to visit the cathedral archives this evening.'

'Don't worry about it,' said Palgrave, who wiped his mouth with his napkin and rose from the table. 'We might be in luck and find it still open. We can have a look there now if you like.'

'Perhaps we ought to wait until tomorrow,' said Shaw.

'I've a rather full day tomorrow,' said Palgrave. 'It won't take a jiffy to have a look round now. Oh, and by the way, this was left for you.'

He took a visiting card from the chimney-piece and handed it to Shaw. It bore the name of Mrs Vale, and carried a hand written inscription asking him to call on her at ten o'clock the following morning.

'A royal summons, eh?' said Palgrave. 'Come along, we'd better hurry before they lock the Chapter House.'

A few minutes later the two men were walking along the darkened cloisters of the cathedral. They approached the door which led into the Chapter House. It was ajar, and when Palgrave touched the handle, it swung open with a slight creak.

'Ah, good,' he said. 'Harris must still be on his rounds or he would have locked up. We're in luck.'

'Is there a risk we may be locked in?' asked Shaw. He felt somewhat uncomfortable wandering around the closed cathedral at night, particularly after his conversation with Gregory and Wheatley.

'No,' said Palgrave, pointing to the lock of the door. 'Look, it's one of those latch affairs. If Harris shuts it we can open it ourselves from inside. Even if we can't, it won't kill us to bed down in the cathedral. Better than that bunker in Cambrai we had to share.'

Shaw realised Palgrave was right, and chastised himself for cowardice. He had been through far worse, and a darkened cathedral with the extremely unlikely possibility of a Russian agent lurking within seemed a laughable thing of which to be afraid.

As they walked along the stone flags of the corridor which led to the main room of the Chapter House, their footsteps echoed throughout the cathedral, and the dim light from Palgrave's battery torch cast eerie shadows on the ancient walls. There was the smell of wood smoke in the air. Shaw assumed it must come from the first fires of autumn in the Cathedral Close houses, which enjoyed some ancient right of wood-gathering which meant they did not have to buy coal.

There was something unsettling about it, and he realised the last time he had smelled wood smoke in a church it had been in a bombed-out monastery chapel on the Western Front in which he had held a service of midnight mass on Christmas Eve, 1917.

There had been something vaguely obscene in the sight of the huge, smouldering crucifix which lay in the rubble where it had fallen from the high altar. The smoke had still drifted up from it like incense, as if everything sacred in the world had been inverted into a parody.

He shuddered. His meeting with Gregory and Wheatley had unsettled him, and he was relieved when Palgrave stopped at a large, studded wooden door. A thin strip of light shone out from its base.

'Hello,' said Palgrave. 'Looks like someone's left the light on.' He turned the handle and walked in, then Shaw heard him exclaim in surprise, 'oh, it's you!'

'Mr Palgrave, and Mr Shaw,' said the man in the room. 'What brings you here at this time of night?'

Dr Adams sat at a large oak table in the middle of a room whose walls were lined with ancient, crumbling leatherbound books, apart from one wall where a huge, ornate mullioned window in the Early English style rose upward to the vaulted ceiling. The only illumination was a small, green-shaded electric lamp on the table, upon which numerous volumes had been scattered.

Shaw and Palgrave exchanged glances.

'Come along,' said Adams. 'You must have a reason'.

'I should rather like to ask you the same question, Dr Adams,' said Palgrave.

Shaw sensed a confrontation, and moved to assuage it. How much, he wondered, should he reveal to the Dean?

'We wish to look into certain…architectural matters connected with the cathedral,' he said.

'They must be very important matters to justify a visit at this time of night,' said Adams.

'As are presumably the matters you are looking into,' countered Palgrave.

Adams chuckled. 'Gentlemen, let's not beat around the bush. I suspect we are both here for the same reason.'

'Which is?' asked Palgrave.

'To ascertain whether or not there is a secret passage leading to the King's Gallery. Am I correct?'

'Indeed you are,' said Shaw. 'But how…?'

'It doesn't take a genius,' said Adams with a sly smile, 'to work out that if – I say *if* – the late Dean was pushed off the balcony, then whoever did it must have got on and off there by some sort of concealed entrance.'

Adams must have noticed the look of surprise on Shaw's face. 'Oh yes, Mr Shaw. You are not the only person to have doubts about the Dean's death. Inspector Wragg told me that he found you and Mr Palgrave on the King's Gallery earlier.'

'He wishes to undertake further investigation, perhaps?' asked Shaw.

'Not a bit of it,' said Adams dismissively. 'He merely asked me to ensure that nobody goes up there to, as he put it, "snoop about". He remains convinced Vale's death was nothing more than an accident. I must confess I am not so sure. So I made some enquiries about the possibility of a secret passage.'

'And?' asked Palgrave.

'And very little came to light,' said Adams. 'Our Clerk of Works is a new man, and has no knowledge of it. His predecessor is retired, and I believe, sadly, has lost his mental faculties. Our oldest Chapter member, Canon Toddington, knows nothing of it. There may be some elderly servants who could help, but I have not had time to search for them. So I came here.'

'Did you find anything?' asked Shaw.

'As Virgil said, "all I know is that I know nothing",' said Adams quizzically.

'That was Socrates,' said Palgrave, with a note of irritation in his voice. 'Did you or didn't you find anything?'

'Have a look at this,' said Adams, who stood up slowly and turned to the shelf behind him. 'These are the volumes which deal with construction works for the cathedral. Scrapbooks of plans, estimates, bills, drawings, and so on.' He ran his finger along the shelf, leaving a slight mark in the thin layer of dust which coated it.

'The King's Gallery was constructed in 1814. Any passage incorporated at that time must surely have been mentioned in the plans. But look here. This is the record book for 1800 to 1810. This is the record book for 1820 to 1830. But the record for 1810 to 1820 ought to be here.'

He pointed to a section on the shelf where there was a three-inch gap between the volumes.

'I have searched everywhere, gentlemen,' said Adams in a weary voice. 'It is not here. Now why would that one particular volume be missing? Of course, I shall speak to the archivist about it as soon as I can, but I am forced to conclude...'

'That somebody does not wish us to see it,' said Shaw.

But who, he thought, was that somebody?

'Thank you for calling on me, Mr Shaw,' said Mrs Vale as she sat opposite the cleric in her drawing room the following morning. 'More tea?'

'Thank you but no,' said Shaw, covering his cup with his hand. 'I trust you are...bearing up, under the circumstances?'

Mrs Vale waved her hand almost dismissively. 'There is

so much to do, I barely have time for grief,' she answered with a smile. 'I expect the shock will hit me at some point.'

'That is entirely normal,' said Shaw. 'If I can be of any assistance…?'

'That is rather why I invited you,' said Mrs Vale. She put down her cup and saucer on a small ornate table next to the sofa, and turned to Shaw. 'Dr Adams, the new Dean, says you are quite the detective. Is that true?'

Shaw sighed. He had been expecting something like this. Mrs Vale was surrounded by clergy, and it was hardly likely she would call on one she did not know for anything as straightforward as spiritual support.

'I have helped the police on several occasions,' he replied. 'That is all. I assume this is about your late husband's death?'

'Quite so,' replied Mrs Vale. 'I am sorry to say I am less than enamoured of our Inspector Wragg. He seems to have written off the case entirely. I wonder if it was *not* an accident.'

'Indeed,' said Shaw. He recalled his clandestine meeting with agents of the state the previous evening, and decided he must tread carefully. 'And what makes you think that?'

'My late husband may have been a fanatic, but he was not a fool,' replied Mrs Vale. 'He knew perfectly well that balcony was unsafe and would not have put himself in danger by going too close to the edge. He was also in perfect health and not subject to dizzy spells or anything of that nature. And before you ask, nor was he the suicidal type.'

'You are suggesting, therefore, that he was pushed,' said Shaw, lacing his fingers together and pressing them to his lips. 'But there was nobody to be seen on the balcony.'

'Nobody to be seen by anyone in the nave,' said Mrs Vale. 'But that does not mean there was nobody there.'

'But how could anyone else have been there without being seen?' asked Shaw.

'Come now, Mr Shaw,' said Mrs Vale. 'The answer is obvious. There must be some sort of secret entrance to the gallery. These old buildings are riddled with such things. Priest-holes, and the like. In fact, I mentioned it to Dr Adams, and he promised to check in the archives to see if it was mentioned in any documents.'

'Ah…I see we have been thinking along similar lines. I visited the archives myself for the same reason, and met Dr Adams there also.'

'And?'

'And, I regret, the relevant documents appear to be missing.'

Mrs Vale frowned.

'That would seem to be rather a suspicious coincidence,' she said.

'Yes,' said Shaw. 'I believe the plans may have been taken in an attempt to prevent others from finding a secret passage. Which of course, strongly suggests that there *is* such a passage.'

Mrs Vale now beamed a smile which lit up the room. 'Why, Mr Shaw, if only we had policemen like you. I believe you have missed your calling.'

Shaw ignored the flattery. 'Let us assume then, that a person or persons unknown was able to gain access to the King's Gallery and…ah…push your late husband over it without being seen. But who would do such a thing? Did he have enemies?'

Mrs Vale smiled again. 'Oh yes. His outspoken political views ensured that. But I do not think it was done for that reason.'

'What then?' asked Shaw.

'Let me show you something,' said Mrs Vale. She took

144

down a group photograph that was hanging above a bureau in the corner of the room and showed it to him. Shaw saw a group of young people on the steps of an ivy-covered building, with the expressions of innocence and joy that one finds only on youthful faces. It was captioned 'International Summer School, Berlin, 1911'.

'That is me,' said Mrs Vale, pointing to a pretty girl in a white summer dress, holding a parasol. 'It was my first visit abroad; I stayed with a German cousin. All a lot of nonsense really. Idealistic youngsters playing at socialism, or what we thought was socialism. For most of us it was an excuse to mingle with the opposite sex without chaperones.'

'I fail to see the connection,' said Shaw.

'That is Eckhart – I mean, Mr Vale,' said Mrs Vale. She pointed to a figure standing at the rear of the group. Shaw immediately recognised the younger version of the late Dean. He could tell the man was handsome, with swept back hair, and well above average height; impeccably dressed in an expensively tailored clerical suit.

'That is where we met,' said Mrs Vale with a wistful smile. 'He had just finished his curacy then, and was beginning what I think of as his "international phase". Consorting with Germans, Russians, Poles, even Hungarians, and embracing everything that was foreign and radical. Look at the faces of the two women next to him,' she continued. 'I have long forgotten their names. They were Jewesses; French, I think. But I have not forgotten their expressions.'

Shaw looked again and could clearly see admiration, perhaps even desire in the faces of the two young women as they looked at the young clergyman next to them. It was an expression he recognised from seeing it countless times on the faces of women as they looked at their beloved during the marriage service.

Mrs Vale took the photograph and replaced it on the wall. 'What I am trying to say, Mr Shaw, is that my late husband was the sort of man that women tended to fall in love with in rather a dramatic way. That was not something that ended with our marriage. If anything, he seemed to become more attractive to them once he was married.'

Shaw cleared his throat awkwardly. 'Forgive me, Mrs Vale...you are saying that your husband was, ah, unfaithful?'

Mrs Vale smiled again; this time there was a hint of brittleness in it. 'Nothing was ever officially proven. But a wife senses these things, and he admitted as much to me himself. What was particularly hurtful was that I do not believe I ever gave him any real cause to...I mean, it's not as if I...' she paused, seeming to check herself. Shaw thought she might be about to cry, and his hand moved in readiness to his top pocket for a handkerchief. But no tears came, and Mrs Vale carried on talking.

'I certainly loved my husband, Mr Shaw, at least at first. But then came the war, and the Bolshevik revolution, and suddenly politics seemed to be something that had real effects and wasn't just about theories. That is when my husband and I began to...diverge.'

Shaw recognised the symptoms of a formerly buttoned-up person who had found a confidante. He generally found it best to keep quiet in such circumstances, and allow the other party free rein to talk.

'I did not come from a wealthy family,' she continued. 'My father was a suburban bank manager; only really one step removed from being in trade. We had a small house in Putney and could barely afford to keep a brougham. Everything had to be scrimped and saved. Eckhart's family, or his "people" as he would have said, were as rich as

Croesus. That's why communism appealed to him, I think. He didn't know what real poverty was. A woman of my background can never really be more than a liberal playing at socialism. We wanted the vote, and we wanted to work in the professions and study in the universities and stand for Parliament, and we gained all that, so what more was there to fight for? True socialism – the Bolshevik sort – means everyone's poor except a few lucky ones at the top. I began to realise that, but Eckhart did not, and that, I think, is when we fell out of love and…others…began to appear.'

There was a pause and Shaw cleared his throat, wondering if he should ask if he might smoke.

'Perhaps I have said too much,' said Mrs Vale finally. 'It seems so hard to gather one's thoughts in a rational way over this sort of thing. "Frailty, thy name is woman", as Shakespeare puts it.'

'Do I take it,' said Shaw, as kindly as he could, 'that you think a…a jealous lover may have killed your husband?'

He took a deep breath, wondering if such a bald statement would be too much for Mrs Vale, but she smiled brightly again.

'It feels so much better when such things are finally out in the open, doesn't it?' she said. 'Yes. Yes, that is *exactly* what I think. And I am much happier that I should be speaking about it with you, Mr Shaw, than that wretched Inspector Wragg, who if he took any interest at all, would probably discuss every sordid detail with other policemen in some dingy office, and then release everything to the newspapers.'

'Is there any particular woman you suspect?' asked Shaw.

Mrs Vale crossed to the bureau again and took out a note which she handed to Shaw. He read it to himself.

My darling
I must speak with you. I shan't let you leave me, whatever the reason. I will meet you in the usual place. Nobody need know.
All my love,
M.

'May I keep this, Mrs Vale?' asked Shaw. 'I should like to study it further.'

'Be my guest,' said Mrs Vale. 'I should rather like to have burned it anyway.'

'Thank you,' said Shaw, and looked at the note again. 'Oh dear,' he said. 'I wonder if "the usual place" was the King's Gallery? There was some sort of altercation, and…'

'And this woman committed what I believe the French call a crime of passion, and pushed my husband off the balcony,' mused Mrs Vale.

'The voluntary…' whispered Shaw.

'What was that?' asked Mrs Vale.

'The organ voluntary, a Bach piece, was particularly loud during that service,' said Shaw. 'Had there been an altercation on the balcony, I doubt anyone would have heard it.'

Shaw felt he must act, but in what way, he could not decide. 'Mrs Vale,' he said after a pause, 'have you any idea who this "M" could be?'

'I have my suspicions,' said Mrs Vale.

'Do you wish to tell me?' asked Shaw.

'Yes, but it is a little difficult. I believe it to be someone you may know.'

Chapter Ten

Mrs Vale stood up and smoothed down her black dress, then smiled again. 'Am I keeping you from anything, Mr Shaw? Your conference lectures, for example?'

'Not at present, Mrs Vale.'

'Very well. Would you follow me, please?'

Mrs Vale led the way through to her husband's study; a gloomy, book-lined room with a view of the mossy back court of the house.

She pointed to a large bureau by the window piled with papers and documents.

'My husband's desk,' she said. 'Please feel free to look through his papers. If there is anything you think may be of relevance, please let me know. I have looked, but perhaps do not have quite your powers of perception.'

After he had been left alone in the study, Shaw felt that strange feeling he had often felt in his professional life; of intruding on someone's private domain, even though that person were deceased. The dead were beyond this world until the Last Day, of that he was certain, but could they, he sometimes wondered, still know in some way what went on in the places they had left?

He shuddered, and dismissed the thought. It was the here and now that mattered at this juncture, not idle theological speculation.

He opened the lid of the large bureau and saw a mass of letters and papers stuffed into various pigeon-holes. Where to start? What, he wondered, was he actually looking for? He rummaged through the piles of papers; much of them were sermon notes, minutes of meetings and so on; some dry official correspondence but nothing one would not expect to find in a Dean's desk; certainly no *billets doux* or anything remotely incriminating.

He then searched the two drawers under the desk; nothing, except some stationery supplies. He ran his hand along the tops of the pigeon-holes; he had heard that these old desks sometimes had a secret drawer opened by a hidden mechanism. No secret mechanism was operated but his fingers felt something which had been secreted between the top of the pigeon-holes and the desk. He prised it out carefully; it was a letter, and had been opened.

He read through the letter briefly, which was from a well known and venerable firm of Midchester solicitors. Shaw read it out loud to himself softly.

'To the Very Reverend E.T.D. Vale,
Sir
With reference to your letter of the 3rd inst; I will be glad to be of assistance in the matter of the debts contracted by your wife. Kindly call at or telephone to our office to make an appointment,

I remain, yours etc etc…'

Did Mrs Vale know about this, he wondered? She claimed to have already searched the desk, but had she seen that letter? Presumably the matter of her debts was serious, or why seek legal advice? Did it even have any relevance to the matter in hand? He could hardly raise the matter with her in polite conversation, and decided to carefully replace the letter where he had found it.

He wondered whether to begin searching through the papers again, and then stopped. It had been staring him in the face for the whole time and he had not even noticed it. Lying flat on top of the bureau was a large, faded ledger. It was the missing volume from the cathedral archives.

He snatched it up quickly and leafed through its faded, crumbling pages to one which had been marked with a piece of paper. With trembling hands he held up the book to the light and examined an ancient architect's plan of the King's Gallery, dated 1814. In small, immaculate lettering a portion of the plan was marked 'Staircase to ext; (concealed).'

He then almost jumped as the study door opened and Mrs Vale entered. He put the ledger back on the bureau and closed the lid.

'Have you found anything that might suggest foul play?' asked Mrs Vale.

Shaw was momentarily stumped at how to answer that question truthfully.

'I doubt there is anything that would be of interest to Inspector Wragg,' he said carefully.

'Oh well,' said Mrs Vale with a sigh. 'I suppose it was rather a forlorn hope to expect anything. In that case, perhaps the only other avenue left to explore is that of my late husband's, shall we say, romantic interest. If it is of any use, I ought to tell you her name. It is Millicent Reynolds.'

'A wonderful piece, madame,' said the jeweller in a wheedling voice with an accent which might have come from anywhere between Moscow and the Mile End Road. He put the necklace down and removed his eyepiece. 'Eighteen carat gold and genuine diamonds. Such things in Shoreditch we *don't* often see. May I ask…where you got it?'

'No you may not, dear,' said the blowsy woman briskly. 'I was given to understand that the gentleman who gave it to me telephoned to say I was coming.'

'Of course, of course,' said the man with a smile and a shrug of the shoulders which suggested a conspiratorial agreement. He bolted the door of the dark little trinket shop in its dark little corner of east London, and the sounds of horses' hooves and costermongers' cries on the road outside were muted out.

'For *special* customers, madame, privacy we make sure of.'

'How much?' said the blowsy woman.

'Well…' The man shrugged his shoulders again. 'For something so *rare* as this, what you might call *highly sought after*…'

'Look Ikie,' said the woman with a hint of irritation. 'We both know the score so just tell me straight, there's a dear.'

'A hundred guineas,' said the man with a brittle smile which showed the hint of a gold tooth. 'And my name is Yakov.'

'Hmm,' said the woman. 'Worth double that I should think, but as you say, a lot of people are after something like that and some of them wear blue uniforms. I'll take it.'

She tapped her fingers nervously on the little counter as the man peeled out twenty large, white, five pound notes, licking his thumb liberally as he did so.

'There,' said Yakov triumphantly as he patted the notes

into place. 'One hundred pounds.'

'Guineas, you said,' snapped the woman. 'That's a hundred and five quid.'

'Commission,' said Yakov with a leer. 'Take it or leave it.'

'You thieving old…'

'Madame, enough already,' said the jeweller firmly, raising his hands in a placatory gesture. 'The only thief is the person who got this necklace for nothing. Oh, and by the way, just to make sure I have the right lady what I was told about in advance on the telephone by the, ah, previous owner, what is your good name, Miss…?'

'You can just call me Queenie.'

Yakov seemed satisfied, and Queenie, deftly hiding the money on her person as skilfully as a conjuror, left the shop.

Well, that's that, she thought, as she entered a little public house nearby in order to celebrate her good fortune. Given a necklace worth a hundred quid and sent off to make her own way in the world. Fancy her thinking Skinner had killed that Dean chappie in the cathedral! He'd explained it all, and told her she had to clear off, back to London, for her own sake in case the police got involved. Well, she didn't need any more telling after that.

And fancy her thinking he was going to strangle her when she felt his hands round her neck! She never expected he was putting a necklace on her as a leaving present; one he'd been given in lieu of gambling debts, and which was too hot to pawn in Midchester.

That was the most romantic thing a man's done for me, she thought. She'd miss old Skinny. He was a nice sort really. But then again, she pondered, one man's much the same as any other. And with a hundred pounds, she could make an honest living for herself. Get a gown shop, or perhaps even a little guest house of her own.

She smiled back at the well-dressed gent beside her at the bar who gave her a sly grin and touched the brim of his hat.

'Like a drink miss?' he asked.

'Don't mind if I do dear. A port and lemon, please.'

Oh well, she thought. Here we go again. There was always time for an honest living later.

Shaw's head was in a spin following the findings at Vale's desk and the revelation by his widow. He closed the lid of the desk and turned to face Mrs Vale.

'You are certain it was Millicent, I mean, Mrs Reynolds that was…ah…involved, with your late husband?' he asked.

'As certain as one can be,' answered Mrs Vale.

'Based on what, may I ask?'

Mrs Vale frowned. 'You may think me overly possessive, but once I noticed my husband was receiving letters from a woman, I started watching him. From the window, I mean. One can see quite a lot of the cathedral precincts from the upper stories of this building, and I have little else with which to occupy my time.'

'And you saw your husband with…the other woman,' said Shaw.

'Not exactly, no,' said Mrs Vale in a matter-of-fact voice. 'But I did see *her* going to him for one of their trysts.'

Shaw swallowed. 'Trysts?' he asked cautiously.

'My late husband was quite open in telling me he had been meeting another woman,' said Mrs Vale. 'He claimed it was all over and felt the need to confess it. He told me they sat together in the cathedral for services.'

'But surely,' said Shaw, 'that would have been tantamount to an admission of scandal. People would have talked if they were seen together frequently.'

'I did not say anybody *saw* them sitting together,' said Mrs Vale.

'Wait,' said Shaw. 'You mean…that was the reason for the Dean to sit so often in the King's Gallery instead of in the choir?'

'From what my husband told me, yes,' said Mrs Vale. 'He almost taunted me with it, despite claiming to want my forgiveness. He said there was some sort of seating arrangement there whereby a person could not be seen from the nave.'

Shaw's eyes flicked to the cathedral ledger that lay on the top of the late Dean's desk. He made his next statement with a certain degree of caution.

'But Mrs Reynolds would have been seen climbing and descending the spiral staircase to the gallery. Unless….'

'Unless there were another way in and out,' said Mrs Vale. 'Have you come to a similar conclusion?'

'Indeed yes,' said Shaw. He pointed to the dusty volume on the Dean's desk.

'This ledger shows that a secret staircase exists,' he said slowly.

'Exactly,' said Mrs Vale brightly. 'A staircase leading from the cathedral grounds to the King's Gallery and the roof above. It was some sort of secret exit provided in the event of civil tumult, I believe. I myself have never seen it, but like you I reasoned that there must be something of the sort. How my husband knew of it, I do not know. But I assumed some sort of plans of it must exist. I could not ask anybody, of course, for risk of exposing the scandal. That is why I borrowed the ledger from the archives, and sure enough, the passage is shown on the plans.'

'Mrs Vale, why did you not mention that it was you that borrowed the ledger, when I mentioned it earlier?'

Mrs Vale chuckled. 'You will think it rather childish of me but I suppose I was testing you. To see just how observant you are. I left it on my husband's desk to see if you would notice it. I am pleased to see that you did.'

'I see,' said Shaw. 'May I assume that no such "tests" will occur again, and that we may trust one another?'

'We may,' said Mrs Vale. 'I can see that you have considerable powers of observation. Please continue.'

'Very well,' said Shaw. 'Whoever killed your husband, if indeed he *was* killed, must have used that staircase. And if Mrs Reynolds were in the habit of using it...'

'It does appear rather suspicious,' said Mrs Vale.

'And you saw Mrs Reynolds entering this staircase?' asked Shaw.

'No. But I did see her – the Reynolds woman – wandering around the grounds on several occasions before Evensong. One can see quite clearly from the little dormer window of the spare bedroom, but that window is in turn almost impossible to see from the ground, so one can watch the comings and goings without detection. If anyone came into view, she would pretend to be looking at the graves, and then when the way was clear, she would disappear behind a buttress. I expect that was when she went through some sort of hidden door.'

'But you did not see such a door?' asked Shaw.

'Alas no,' said Mrs Vale. 'It is impossible to see the north side of the cathedral from here.'

A thought suddenly struck Shaw. 'What...what was Mrs Reynolds wearing on these occasions?'

'Wearing?' asked Mrs Vale. 'Why, it never particularly occurred to me to notice. She always seemed rather plainly dressed. Mannish, almost. Yes, that's it. Mannish. She usually wore a raincoat – the rubber sort, you know, the type worn for riding that never seems completely clean. And a tweed cap. From a distance one might almost mistake her for a young man or a youth.'

Could this have been the figure he had seen around the cathedral?, thought Shaw. Now that Cyril Peach had been ruled out, it was certainly a possibility.

'Forgive me Mrs Vale,' said Shaw, 'but how did you know it was Mrs Reynolds? I mean to say, had you met her previously, in order to be able to recognise her from a distance?'

'Oh yes,' said Mrs Vale. 'Our paths had crossed. She was connected with some of the charitable work done here at the cathedral – I assume that is how she met my husband – and I had visited her on one or two occasions. So I recognised her quite easily.'

'The police ought to be informed...' said Shaw, and immediately regretted it. He recalled his meeting with Major Wheatley and the Superintendent, and wondered just how much he ought to be telling them.

'It would be a waste of time,' said Mrs Vale with a sudden burst of anger. 'I already mentioned my suspicions about Mrs Reynolds, and the secret passage to Inspector Wragg, who appeared not to be interested other than to tell me not to mention it to anyone else, and merely said he would "get round to having a look into it" at some point. I wondered perhaps...'

'Perhaps I should investigate?' asked Shaw.

'Precisely,' said Mrs Vale, her voice becoming calmer. 'I have no affinity for this sort of thing. I know it sounds feeble, but I dislike small spaces intensely. But if you could spare the time, I would be much obliged. If the existence of a secret stairway could be proven, it would force the police to take a proper interest. And if Mrs Reynolds *is* somehow involved…well then, something ought to be done.'

Shaw wondered just how happy the Suffolk Constabulary would be if he were to make himself known to them again, but he decided to accept the request.

'I shall have a look with Mr Palgrave this afternoon,' said Shaw. 'And I will visit Mrs Reynolds. I cannot of course, confront her in any way.'

'Of course not,' said Mrs Vale. 'But thank you so much for your assistance. My husband and I…had our differences…but if he really was killed by a jealous woman – and I don't for a moment accuse anyone – then something must be done. Quite frankly I do not think a provincial coroner's' inquest will be sufficiently thorough.'

Shaw got up to go. 'May I take this with me?' he asked, lifting the ledger off the desk.

'Of course,' said Mrs Vale. 'Do keep me informed of what you find.'

Shaw shook her proffered hand briefly and hurried out of the Deanery.

'Do pay attention, Redding,' said Palgrave with a note of irritation in his voice. 'It's a G *sharp*, not a flat, on the responses. And do *look* at me. I'm not waving my arms around just to keep the flies off.'

The other boys in the music room tittered. Palgrave always found the Upper Sixth a bit of a trial; now that their voices had broken most of them were only fit for the back row of the cathedral choir and would never get a chance to shine as soloists.

'I'm sorry sir,' said Redding. 'But you always say we

ought to look at the score *and* at you. I don't see how one can do both.'

Palgrave sighed. 'The good Lord gave you eyeballs that can move around for a reason. Look at me, boy. Look up at me, then down at the score. Up at me, down at the score. Up, down, up down.' He rolled his eyes in exaggerated fashion. 'Pretend you're watching a tennis match sideways on.'

There was more laughter and he drowned it out with a chord on the piano. 'Now then,' he roared, 'let's try it again.' He then continued with the Lesser Litany, part of the sung prayers for Evensong.

'"Give peace in our time O Lord…,"' he sang lustily.

Only a feeble response was half-sung by the boys and Palgrave angrily played a dischord and looked up.

'What on earth is the matter with you all today?'

'Please sir,' said one of the boys. 'It's Dr Adams. He's having a fight with someone.'

Palgrave stood up and looked round to the leaded window through which the boys were staring and pointing. Sure enough, Adams was on the lawn shouting and gesticulating at a small, rat-like man in a raincoat and tweed cap who stood next to him in a defiant stance.

'That's old Skinny, the bookie!' shouted one of the boys, who at 17 already sported a small moustache and heavily brilliantined hair. 'Probably owes the Dean money for a horse!'

There were more gales of laughter.

'Silence!' yelled Palgrave, and the boys, used to his rather placid nature, recoiled in shock.

'Sit down and open your psalters at Psalm 113,' he said rapidly, 'and any boy who fails to pitch the opening note on my return will get fifty lines. Merrick, as prefect you are in charge.'

A quiet, responsible looking boy nodded at him and Palgrave strode out of the music room, his black gown flapping behind him.

A few moments later he reached Adams on Cathedral Green. The smaller man saw him approach and scuttled off, soon disappearing into the trees on the far side of the lawn.

'Is everything all right, sir?' asked Palgrave, who used the polite form of address to his superior when within earshot of his pupils.

Adams was red in the face and breathing heavily. He looked round and scowled.

'Oh, it's you, Palgrave. Yes, quite all right, thank you.'

'Should I call the beadles?'

'No need. No need.'

Adams fumbled with a packet of cigarettes and broke a match trying to light one.

'Allow me sir,' said Palgrave, deftly striking a match and lighting Adams' cigarette. He inhaled deeply and seemed to become calmer.

'What was it all about?'

'A ne'er do well, Palgrave. One of the racing fraternity. Name of Skinner.'

'A bookie?'

'Quite so. We've had trouble with him before, hanging around the place. Taking bets from some of the minor canons, even some of the wives in the Close, would you believe it? Of course, you're relatively new and it was a bit before your time.'

'Disgraceful,' said Palgrave.

'Indeed. Then we had the business with Cyril Peach and the death of the late Dean. As if we haven't enough on our plates. When I saw him I warned him off but he became abusive. I'm glad you came out when you did. One never

160

knows if these types will cut up rough.'

'That's quite all right sir. Ought we to inform the police?' asked Palgrave.

'We tried before,' said Adams, 'but the Green is technically public land and unless a constable or one of the beadles catches him *in flagrante* there is not much to be done. Skinner knows it and usually makes sure he's not seen.'

'I'll keep an eye out for him, sir,' said Palgrave. 'But now I ought to be getting back to the Upper Sixth. We are attempting an anthem by Orlando Gibbons but the only gibbons that lot know are the ones in Midchester Zoo.'

Adams laughed weakly and puffed on his cigarette.

'Ah, Palgrave…I should be grateful if you did not discuss Skinner with the boys. The parents, you know…we have already had so much scandal.'

'Of course sir. I'll be getting along.'

'Oh and Palgrave, has your friend Mr Shaw made any advances in his, ah, investigation?'

'Not as far as I know, sir.'

Palgrave paused for a moment and then took a deep breath before continuing. 'On that topic, sir, may I ask why you told the under-organist to pay that Bach piece for the voluntary at Evensong on the day of the Dean's death?'

Adams threw Palgrave a frosty glance, and trod his cigarette into the lawn.

'I fail to see the relevance.'

'Only the late Dean favoured quiet pieces for the voluntary. I just thought…'

'You just thought a little too much on the topic, Palgrave, said Adams with a smile. 'I have always felt that Evensong ought to end on a note of cheerfulness and optimism, such as that provided by the Bach piece in question. Prior to my…dispute…with the late Dean, I deferred to his choice of more reflective pieces, but decided on that occasion to over-rule him, as was my right. It was a rather silly little attempt at revenge.'

'I see,' said Palgrave. 'Well, I'd better be getting back.' As if to underscore the point, there was a crash of a desk lid and a roar of laughter from the direction of the music room.

'Quite so, Palgrave,' said Adams as he turned to go. 'And do keep me informed of Mr Shaw's progress, won't you?'

Shaw delivered his last lecture, which was received politely but without much enthusiasm by the other delegates. There was now only one day left of the conference, and after that he was required to return to Lower Addenham to resume his parish duties. As he walked out of Diocesan House during the lunch break, he wondered about the revelations made by Mrs Vale. Could the Dean's death be connected in some way with Mrs Reynolds, or was it just the over-active imagination of a jealous wife? Ought he to mention it to Palgrave?

There was so little go to on…and yet, somehow, in the back of his mind, he felt that wheels were turning and facts were being sifted in some unconscious way. He decided to put off the matter until he had had a chance to investigate the secret staircase to the King's Gallery.

To that end, he walked around the cathedral grounds to the north wall. He had brought the ledger in his rucksack, and took it out to consult the faded plan and elevation of the structure. There was no depiction of the outer wall, but by his reckoning, the stairwell must be concealed inside the large pillar which ran down the outside of the north transept. There was nowhere else it could be, as large windows were on either side of the gallery.

He picked his way through the tussocky grass; there were various tombstones and monuments in the grounds, all of which seemed at least fifty years old; he surmised that any more recent burials would have taken place in Midchester Cemetery. Finally he reached the pillar on the north wall and stared upwards; the ancient stone seemed to soar hundreds of feet into the air, as sheer as a sea cliff. There was no sign of a door; of course, he thought, there would not be, as the passage would not then be a secret.

There was, however, a large memorial slab against the foot of the pillar, at least six feet high, covered in moss. Shaw looked at the barely legible inscription. There appeared to be no name on it, but only two lines of text:

SIC SEMPER TYRANNIS
St Matthew ch.7 V.14

Underneath that was the depiction in bas relief of a skull and a broken bone; a femur perhaps.

Shaw stared for a moment in puzzlement. He was familiar with the Latin motto, 'thus always to tyrants', said to have been uttered by Julius Caesar's assassin. But he did not recognise the Biblical text. He reached into his coat for the tiny pocket Bible he always carried with him. He leafed through it until he came to the relevant chapter, and raised his eyebrows when he read it.

'Strait is the gate, and narrow is the way which leadeth unto life, and few there be that find it.'

This must be some sort of secret passage, he thought. The lack of a name on a tombstone was odd, and the mention of tyrants…could that refer to Napoleon? He looked again at the depiction of the skull, and the bone broken apart.

Of course, thought Shaw, and he laughed out loud. A 'bone apart'. Napoleon Bonaparte! It was a cryptic reference, a little joke of the type favoured by cathedral craftsmen in times past. The King's Gallery had been built to honour the men who had united to defeat Napoleon. It must be a way in!

Looking cautiously behind to make sure he was unobserved, Shaw felt all around the stone, pushing and pressing in various places, but nothing happened. Then he felt the entire stone wobble, and he realised the slab was on some sort of pivot. There were signs that moss had been cleared around the bottom, top and right hand edges, but not on the left.

He clawed with his fingers between the edge of the slab and the wall, and then the 'door' suddenly rolled open, counterbalanced by its own weight. There was a rush of escaping, musty air and a dark passage opened up before him, with a flight of steps leading steeply upwards.

'It's astonishing!' said Palgrave, as he and Shaw walked from the Cathedral Close to the entrance to the secret passage. 'To think, it's been here all these years, and nobody knew about it.'

Shaw had decided not to enter the passage alone; partly because he wanted a witness with him if anything important should be discovered, and partly, if he were honest, because he was somewhat fearful. Fortunately, Palgrave, whom he met at the house, had a free period and so they decided to investigate before returning for lunch.

There was something about the pitch-black passageway that was, if not exactly sinister, then un-nerving. Besides, he had no means of lighting his way other than a few matches, but he knew Palgrave kept a battery torch at home.

'You were right to wait,' said Palgrave. 'The entire Third Form were trooping past here earlier on a nature walk and you might have been seen. Much better to do it now when things are quieter.'

Shaw showed Palgrave the memorial slab against the north wall and pointed out the inscription.

'Well, well,' chuckled Palgrave. 'Fancy that. Mind you, it's the sort of thing you wouldn't give a second glance at if seen from a distance. Of course, that would be the point. If the Tsar had had to make a quick getaway, a carriage could have been kept nearby and he could have been whisked away to safety without any of the mob seeing him.'

'And it is not particularly easy to open,' said Shaw. 'It took some effort to do so. I suspect that is why so few people knew about it.'

'Well, lead the way, Lord Carter,' joked Palgrave. 'Let's see what's inside King Tut's tomb, shall we?'

Shaw, with some effort, eased open the slab and Palgrave shone his torch up the steps. The beam of the electric light did not lessen the sinister aspect of the staircase; it seemed to make it worse, revealing long, dust-laden cobwebs and several large spiders which scuttled away into the dark.

Palgrave must have caught the look of distaste on Shaw's face. He grinned and mounted the steps.

'I'll go first. Can't be any worse than going over the top.'

After closing the heavy door behind them, the two men made slow progress up the steep winding steps; there were no handholds and only small alcoves set into the stone at regular intervals, which Shaw assumed had been carved to house lanterns.

'Look,' said Palgrave, shining his torch on the steps. 'Footmarks. Looks like someone's been in here fairly recently. I suppose we ought not to disturb them – they may be evidence.'

'We have no other way of ascertaining whether they *are* evidence, unless we investigate further,' said Shaw.

'You're right,' said Palgrave. 'Come on then.'

After what seemed like a long time, although it was probably less than a minute, the staircase opened out into a small vestibule with a wood-panelled wall.

'This must be the entrance to the gallery,' said Palgrave. 'Yes, look, you can see the catch to the door quite clearly here.' He pointed to a rusty metal latch set into the panelling. 'Of course, there would be no point in hiding it on this side.'

Palgrave, using his handkerchief to protect any fingerprints which might be on the handle, gently eased open the door a crack and looked out.

'That's it all right,' he whispered, closing the door quietly, and resuming in his normal voice. 'You were right about there being a secret door in the panelling on the gallery, but I expect we had no way of finding it from there. It was probably built so that it could only be opened on this side.'

'That would make sense,' said Shaw. 'A bodyguard would have been posted inside, to open the door if required. The lack of an exterior handle would impede the progress of anybody who mounted the King's Gallery and tried to pursue the escaping Tsar.'

'They thought of everything, the Machiavellian rogues,' said Palgrave. 'Here, let me have a look at those plans.'

Shaw handed Palgrave the ledger, and held the battery torch while he leafed through the pages.

'That's it,' he said, pointing to the plan of the gallery. 'Bang on. This is where we are. "'Staircase to ext; (concealed)".'

'Quite so, but where does this lead?' asked Shaw. He had noticed that the staircase continued round upwards to the right, away from the panelling.

'Hmm,' said Palgrave, poring over the plans. 'Nothing about it on here. Only one way to find out.'

They carefully mounted the steep staircase, which was narrower than it had been further down. The roof seemed to become lower, and Shaw had a sudden vision of being trapped in some tiny stone coffin, but it soon passed as the staircase ended abruptly at a wooden ceiling.

'It's a trap door,' said Palgrave, prodding the spongy wood. 'Look, there's a latch.'

With some effort he dislodged the rusty metal latch and pushed gently at the timbers, which lifted upwards, flooding the chamber with early evening sunlight.

'I say, it's the roof,' said Palgrave, sticking his head out into the sunshine. 'Why on earth didn't anyone know about this?'

The two men clambered out on to the leaded roof of the cathedral, into a world of sunlight, space and air. Gingerly, Shaw stood up, relieved to see that a stone balustrade about three feet high guarded the edges. Then, towering above them, he saw the enormous soaring spire of the cathedral, casting its shadow on to part of the roof.

'Nobody's used this for ages,' said Palgrave, brushing the remains of long-abandoned birds' nests from the timber door. 'I doubt anyone's even been up here since the last quinquennial inspection, which must be nearly five years ago now. The Clerk of Works' predecessor lost his marbles apparently, so probably didn't even know about it.'

'I assume it is almost impossible to see it, concealed behind these buttresses,' said Shaw, looking around him. 'But why hide it? Surely no assassins of the Tsar would be lurking on the roof.'

'No, I think it's older than that,' mused Palgrave. 'I think that staircase has been here a lot longer. A priest hole perhaps, something the Catholics built to hide their lot during the persecutions. I think the chaps who built the King's Gallery adapted it, after all, you could hardly expect them to build a huge stone staircase like that just for one royal visit.'

'You are probably right,' said Shaw, 'which is why the exit to the roof is not mentioned on the plans. It was not part of the proposed escape route, and therefore not relevant.'

'But it would have been handy for a priest if he couldn't risk getting out via the ground floor,' mused Palgrave. 'He could just come up here and wait until the Reformers had passed on.'

There was silence for a moment as the two men gazed out on the view; below them was Cathedral Green, the few passers-by and motor cars visible looking for all the world like pieces from a model railway set; beyond lay Midchester and then the rolling Suffolk countryside, a sheet of harvest gold leading all the way to a thin sliver of light on the horizon where the sun glinted on the North Sea.

'This does at least prove it was possible for an assailant to push Mr Vale off the King's Gallery, and make his escape undetected,' said Shaw.

'Yes,' mused Palgrave, 'and he must have got out via the ground floor. I don't think there's any other way down except through the tower – there's a door there which leads out on to the roof, I remember from when I've been up it a couple of times – but the tower staircase comes out right by the west door where the beadle sits. Anyone trying to escape through there would have been noticed.'

'Unless he simply concealed himself in the staircase until the way was clear,' said Shaw.

'Yes, well, there is that I suppose,' said Palgrave. 'The cove might still be lurking in some hidden corner of the staircase at this very moment for all we know. But at any rate, Inspector Wragg ought to have the decency to give you a hearing now we know our theory is workable. We should get back before someone notices,' he added.

The two men made their way carefully down the stone steps; as before, Palgrave led the way, picking out the route with the narrow beam of his torch.

Shaw realised he was dreading having to mention what Mrs Vale had told him about the man's sister. Ought he even mention it to him? Perhaps, he thought, it would be better to keep silent.

Shaw's internal monologue was suddenly and violently disturbed when he heard a loud cry from Palgrave, who had steadied himself by putting a hand in one of the niches in the wall.

'My God, Shaw, look at this….'

Chapter Eleven

Palgrave finished the last of a stiff whisky that Shaw had poured for him on their return to the house. 'That's the ticket – thanks old man,' he said, and looked down at the object on the table. 'I still can't believe it,' he said.

'I am afraid there is little doubt about it,' said Shaw. 'That is your sister's cap.'

The object in question looked harmless enough on the table, but, found in an alcove by the scene of a possible murder, it had taken on a decidedly suspicious aspect.

'Look, as I mentioned before,' said Shaw, turning the cap in his hands, 'here is her name written clearly in ink on the lining.'

'Common,' said Palgrave. 'That's what Winnie, our maid of all work, would say about a name inked on clothing. Ought to have been a proper label, sewn in. I expect sis didn't think it was worth the bother. She's always losing caps and scarves and things on that blasted horse of hers, and probably hoped if found they would be sent back.'

Shaw looked again and raised an eyebrow.

'Oh dear,' he said.

'What now?'

'I almost missed them. Two hairs trapped in the inner band. Blonde.'

'Not much doubt about it then. It's hers,' said Palgrave.

'But what on earth was it doing in there?'

Shaw took a deep breath. 'I'm sorry to have to break it to you, Palgrave, but your sister was…ah…involved with Vale.'

'Involved? You mean she…?'

'It seems so. When I spoke to Mrs Vale she was quite open about it, and showed me a…communication, signed "M"'. The letter suggested Vale wished to break off the affair, and Millicent – if indeed it was her – was unhappy about it and suggested a meeting at the usual place.'

'Dash it all, Shaw,' said Palgrave angrily. 'Why didn't you tell me this before?'

'I was waiting for the right time. I had hoped it would not be necessary at all, but now…'

'Thanks. Thoughtful of you,' said Palgrave, 'and I don't mean to sound angry with you. It's just a bit of a shock…by the way, what's this "usual place" mentioned in the letter?'

'According to Mrs Vale, your sister and her husband sat together on the King's Gallery at services, where she could sit near him and not be seen by anyone else.'

'That's just the sort of bally silly thing she would do,' said Palgrave. 'She was always furtive, even as a kiddie. Playing tricks on the servants, and so on. And getting involved with a married man, well, that's a surprise but when I think about it isn't really. It's just the sort of romantic novelist's idea she'd fall for.'

There was a pause and Palgrave looked into his empty glass.

'I say Shaw, you don't think…I mean, could she have…if Vale was breaking things off and…well…"hell hath no fury like a woman scorned", and all that.'

'You are suggesting your sister may have been involved in some way with Vale's death?' asked Shaw carefully.

'I don't know what to think,' replied Palgrave. 'I think she never got over her husband's death, you know. Sort of idolised him and never found any man that could measure up. Then she finally finds one she likes, he's married but she doesn't mind, perhaps hopes he'd leave his wife, but then he throws her over and…well, she throws him over in return. Possibly literally.'

'Is that likely?' asked Shaw. 'I barely know your sister.' He could not help thinking of the half-glimpsed figure in beige he had seen on the King's Gallery before Vale had fallen to his death.

'She's always been headstrong and impulsive,' replied Palgrave. 'And lately, all this socialism business. Not having children eventually makes some women turn a bit peculiar, in my experience.'

'But it does not make them murderers,' said Shaw quietly.

'Well I've a good mind to cycle over to the old place and have it out with her this instant,' said Palgrave, standing up quickly. 'And don't tell me we ought to go to the police. I'd rather hear what she has to say first.'

'I agree entirely, and I shall come with you,' said Shaw quickly.

'What on earth for?' said Palgrave as he shrugged on his jacket.

'As, ah…moral support. For both of you.'

'You're right of course, Shaw,' said Palgrave. 'Of course you must come. Thanks for the offer.'

Shaw did not like to mention that he had had some experience of confronting murder suspects, and he had learned to his cost it was not something that ought to be done alone.

'Never understood why she wore that thing anyway,' said Palgrave, looking down at the cap. 'Made her look like a stable boy or a bookie's runner...wait!'

Palgrave had almost shouted the last word of his sentence, and Shaw looked up in alarm.

'Yes?'

'Bookie's runner,' said Palgrave. 'In all the excitement about the secret passage, I clean forgot.'

'Something of importance?'

'Possibly. I witnessed an altercation this morning between Adams, and a shifty looking chap who turned out to be a bookie. Name of Skinner. Sort of...rattish looking man, you know, runty, but the type who makes up for it by acting the "tough guy", as they say in the films. At any rate, I learned from Adams, and some of the minor canons I quizzed about it later in the common room, that the fellow is often hanging about, taking bets and paying out winnings.'

'To clergy? Surely that is not permitted?' said Shaw.

'Strictly speaking no, but as Adams said, the Green and the Close are public land and he can't easily be stopped unless a copper catches him. Hangs about at all hours apparently.'

'What does he look like, this fellow?' asked Shaw.

'As I said, ratty. Thin, about five and a half feet tall. Little moustache.'

'No, I mean, what type of clothing does he wear?'

'Oh, I see. Well, you know, macintosh, and, well, a cap like that one on the table.'

'I see,' mused Shaw. 'I wonder if it is he who has been loitering in the precincts at night, especially since the original suspect, Cyril Peach, has been discounted.'

'Most likely,' said Palgrave. 'I'm new enough at the cathedral not to have known about all this but it seems flutters on the horses are quite the thing round here. One of the canons said Skinner was even hanging around the

Dean's house. When it was Vale living there, I mean. Well if I see him again, he'll feel my boot. I don't object to betting but I don't like his sort hanging around with impressionable youngsters in the vicinity. People seem to forget off-course betting is illegal, as well, but it's one of those things people wink at, like a bit of poaching.'

'Do you happen to know where this…person… might be found?' asked Shaw.

'No idea. I say, *you* don't want to put a bet on a horse, do you?' asked Palgrave incredulously.

'Gambling has never interested me,' said Shaw. 'But he may have seen something. Such types often have an "ear to the ground", as they say, and are not likely to speak to the police about what they know.'

'And you think you'll get something out of him?' asked Palgrave. 'Well good luck, assuming you can find him.'

Suddenly there was the noise of a plate breaking in the kitchen. The two men looked at each other in alarm, and after a second's pause, Palgrave put a finger to his lips and crept to the fireplace. Silently he lifted the poker, and in one move threw open the kitchen door to reveal a terrified woman leaning suspiciously close to the keyhole of the door.

'Oh it's you Mrs S,' said Palgrave, lowering the improvised weapon. 'I thought you were a burglar.'

'I'm sorry sir,' said Mrs Snelgrove as she straightened up. 'I just come in to do your lunch, and I heard voices, and I didn't like to interrupt, then I noticed the door knob needed a bit of a clean, like.'

Palgrave chuckled. 'I trust the door knob is spick and span now. I'm sorry if I scared you but with all the goings on around here lately, I'm a bit on edge. Just what did you hear?'

'I was just coming in, sir, when I heard the name of

Skinner.'

Shaw caught a look of relief on Palgrave's face and realised it was unlikely that Mrs Snelgrove had heard anything about Millicent. He discretely covered the cap on the table with a nearby newspaper.

'Ah...our mysterious bookie,' said Palgrave. 'Don't tell me you're a gambling addict?'

'Certainly not sir,' said the servant with a sniff. 'I was raised Baptist. But Mr Snelgrove likes...well I don't like to say it in front of a man of the cloth, like.'

'It's quite all right, Mrs S,' said Palgrave. 'Shaw's a decent sort and won't have your husband excommunicated just for a flutter now and then.'

'Well...' continued Mrs Snelgrove doubtfully, 'He *does* like a wager from time to time, and his, as you might say, "agent" for that is Mr Skinner. And my Bert – that is, Mr Snelgrove, he told me as to look out for him, as he owes him money.'

'Wait a minute, Mrs Snelgrove,' said Palgrave. 'Who owes money to whom?'

'That Skinner owes my Bert – Mr Snelgrove, that is – money for a horse what came in the other day. But of course when he – that is, Mr Skinner – owes someone money, he's nowhere to be seen. Now my Bert...'

'That is, your Mr Snelgrove,' interrupted Palgrave with a smile.

'That's right, my Bert, well he gave me the slip.'

'You mean he eluded you?' asked Palgrave.

'Eh?' replied Mrs Snelgrove. 'No, I mean he gave me the slip that Mr Skinner writes out if you, ah, engage him, so to speak. If I sees the man I'm to show it to him and get the money. I can't say as I like dealing with his sort, but six bob is six bob, and my Bert can't do it on account of his chest.'

'I fail to see how this if of any use to us, Mrs S,' said Palgrave, 'fascinating though it may be.'

'What I mean to say sir,' replied the domestic, 'is if you has any business with Skinner, though I'm sure I wouldn't know why you would, perhaps you could call in for me on the public house he frequents. If you were passing, that is. The Red Lion, on Dock Lane.'

'That's that shabby little place at the end of the harbour,' said Palgrave. 'I've coxed the school eights past it on the river. Can't say I'd like to visit it on land.'

'I'm sure I don't know,' said Mrs Snelgrove airily. 'It's not the sort of place I like to go to on my own. But I need to get that money for Mr Snelgrove somehow.'

'Look here Mrs S,' said Palgrave, 'I'll get Mr Snelgrove's money for him. You give me that slip and I'll pop down.'

'Oh would you sir? That's very Christian of you,' beamed Mrs Snelgrove. She unfolded a small slip of paper and placed it on the table.

Shaw could not help smiling at the idea that Christian charity extended to collecting gambling winnings. Then his smile disappeared as he looked down at the betting slip.

'Ah, Mrs S, Palgrave,' he said rapidly, 'we ought to begin our lunch. Time is getting on.'

It was unclear if Mrs Snelgrove took the hint or genuinely had other things to do, but she glanced at the clock on the chimney-piece and retreated to the kitchen.

'Goodness you're right sir,' she said as she put on her coat. 'I've the minor canons' luncheon to prepare and here's me gossiping. I've left your food on the dresser. Oh and I expect you'll be stopping my wages for that plate I just broke, sir?'

'Nonsense, Mrs S,' said Shaw jovially. 'Mr Palgrave will

do nothing of the kind. I shall foot the bill for the broken plate. Now, good day to you!'

Shaw bustled a somewhat confused Mrs Snelgrove out of the kitchen door, and bolted it behind her.

'I say, who's master of this house?' asked Palgrave in mock pomposity. 'If I wish to stop the skivvy's wages for a broken plate I shall do so.'

'I'm sorry but I had to get rid of her,' said Shaw in a low voice.

'Why?'

'It's the betting slip. Look at it. All of it, I mean.'

Palgrave squinted at the little piece of paper and read out in a breathless monologue what was written on it. '"Skinny" at the top – these coves don't like to use their real name I suppose – "sixpence, single" – last of the big spenders – "Northern Dream" – daft name for a horse – "2.30 Haydock."' He rubbed his chin then looked back at Shaw.

'I say,' he finally announced. 'It's one of those carbon copy receipt pad things, but it looks awfully like…'

'Like this?' asked Shaw, and took out from his pocket the torn scrap of paper they had found in the King's Gallery. He put it next to the betting slip on the table.

'By George, Shaw, you're a genius,' exclaimed Palgrave rapidly. 'Yes, look, it's the same handwriting, although this is an original, not a carbon copy. But the half where he writes his name and so on was torn off. The rest of it, "ny, le, sin, O, tree," isn't the title of some French riddle. It must be half of a bet.

'Look, "ny" are the last two letters of "Skinny", our bookmaker friend's nickname. And it's not the French word "le", at all, it's "le" as in the last two letters of "single", as in a shilling or sixpence single bet. Then "sin", well, that's probably the last three letters of the name of a

177

horse. Yes! If I recall rightly, there's one called Tamsin, it did well in the Grand National. Even I've heard of that old nag.

'Then "O", well that's easy, it's not an O, it's a naught. Damned silly we don't strike a line through them to avoid confusion, like the French do. Or is it the Swedes? Never mind. Must be a time. Say, 2.30. But what about "tree"? If Skinner always writes his slips in the same order, that ought to be the name of a racecourse.'

'Aintree?' suggested Shaw. 'But that's on the other side of the country.'

'Brilliant!' exclaimed Palgrave. 'But distance is no object, Shaw! These chaps put the orders through by telephone these days. So it *was* a betting slip. Probably torn in half because it didn't win. I've seen people do that in disgust. Whoever dropped that could be the killer.'

'Let us not be too hasty,' said Shaw. 'It could have been dropped by anyone at any time.'

'No it couldn't, Shaw,' said Palgrave excitedly. 'Don't you see – it could only have been dropped there when the fixture, or race, or whatever you call it, was known about. Now I don't know much about this sort of thing but I'll wager it only gets announced in the papers on the day of the race, or perhaps a day or two before, so if we can find out when that race was, we can at least narrow down when that piece of paper was dropped.

'If it turns out Tamsin hasn't run a race at Aintree for six months, well, then I'll accept some errant cleaner or repair man dropped it up in the King's Gallery while skiving off work, but until then I think we can assume whoever dropped that was somehow involved in the recent death of the Dean.'

Shaw thought for a moment, then made a decision. 'I shall visit this Skinner, and find out what he knows, including the date of the Aintree race.'

'I say, Shaw, is that wise?' asked Palgrave with a look of concern on his face. 'The Red Lion looks hardly the sort of place for a parson. The bobbies patrol in pairs down there.'

'I am a minister of the church, not somebody's maiden aunt,' said Shaw. 'Our Lord's ministry was among those rejected by polite society, and it ill behoves me to shrink from a visit to one of the poorer parts of town.'

'Very well,' sighed Palgrave. 'I wouldn't expect any less from someone who insisted on dishing out Holy Communion in the middle of an artillery barrage. But I'm coming with you.'

'I think not,' said Shaw firmly. 'To go in "mob handed", as the saying goes, might attract the, ah, wrong response. I shall simply speak to this man on the pretext of collecting Mr Snelgrove's winnings, and see what, if anything, I can find out. He is hardly likely to find me threatening. After all, how many "copper's narks" wear clerical collars?'

'And what am I supposed to do in the meantime?' asked Palgrave, somewhat petulantly.

'Didn't you say you were playing at Evensong today?' asked Shaw.

'Yes,' replied Palgrave, 'but what about sis? Millicent, I mean. Aren't we going to cycle over there? Surely we ought to be speaking to her as well. If she was involved in some way, she ought to come clean with the police.'

'Very well,' said Shaw. 'Would your sister object if the two of us were to arrive at short notice for dinner tonight? She did say that we might drop in whenever we liked.'

'Good idea,' said Palgrave. 'I'll telephone her straight away, and then tonight we'll find out from her just what on earth is going on. I'll take this.'

Palgrave took the cap and wrapped it carefully in the newspaper which covered it.

'And I shall take these.' Shaw took the betting slips from the table.

'If I don't hear back from you by seven pm,' said Palgrave, 'I shall assume you have either had your throat slit, or that you have converted the entire clientele of the Red Lion and are holding a hymn-singing session.'

Shaw cycled slowly through the dockside district of Midchester. This part of the town had suffered badly from the slump; there were boarded-up workshops and 'no hands wanted' signs on the gates of those still in operation; unemployed men loafed on the street corners and some queued for a soup kitchen at a tin chapel with a sign above the door that proclaimed 'The Lord Will Provide'.

He received suspicious glances when he asked a pair of housewives, meticulously scrubbing the front steps of their shabby houses, the whereabouts of the Red Lion; he suspected it was not the sort of place a clergyman would usually visit.

Finally he came to the place; a small corner pub with grubby net curtains in the windows. He cautiously walked inside. A man in shirt sleeves was sweeping sawdust off the floor into a dustpan. He looked up at Shaw with hostile resignation.

'We're closed,' he said sullenly. 'Afternoon closing time. Come back six o'clock if you want a drink. If you can't wait the grocer down the road'll sell you something'.

'Thank you but I am not here for refreshment,' said Shaw. 'I came to enquire after one of your, ah, customers.

A Mr Skinner.'

'Oh yes?' said the man with a raised eyebrow 'Who's asking?'

'My name is Shaw.'

'What's your business with Sk…Mr Skinner?'

'An, er, acquaintance of mine recently had some good fortune. I have come to collect his winnings.'

The man's face softened a little into the hint of a conspiratorial grin. 'Ah, well that's all right then. We don't get many parsons in here, though some of the young 'uns from the cathedral like a flutter now and then, but they don't like to show their faces down here. I thought perhaps you was some sort of church high-up come to give 'em a ticking orf. Ain't a bishop, are you?'

The man laughed uproariously; Shaw simply smiled.

'Round the back,' said the man, pointing with his thumb. 'Knock three times, else they might think you're a bogie.'

Shaw, vaguely remembering that 'bogie' was slang for a policeman, picked his way along a dank, grease-stained corridor behind the bar to a door with peeling paintwork, upon which he made three gentle knocks.

Instantly it was opened, and a small, slightly built man with rodent-like features wearing a gaudy bow tie looked up at him, a cigarette dangling from his lips.

'If you want the Haydock race you're too late,' he said.

'Mr Skinner?' asked Shaw.

'Yeah. What do you want?' replied the man.

'To collect some winnings.'

'Hmm.' Skinner looked Shaw up and down. 'Don't know you, do I?'

'I am here on behalf of someone else. A Mr Snelgrove.'

'Old Bert, eh? You'd better come in.'

Skinner stood aside and Shaw entered a shabby room with a shuttered window and a dim unshaded electric light bulb hanging from the ceiling. There was a battered table in the corner with a telephone, slips of paper and coins on it.

A bored looking woman with artificially blonde hair sat on a wooden chair nearby, leafing through a cinema magazine; she glanced up momentarily, looked Shaw up and down with a professional eye, then, presumably seeing no business opportunity, returned to her reading.

A small wireless set on a high shelf was blaring out dance-band music. Skinner turned down the volume.

'You from the cathedral?' asked Skinner.

'Temporarily, yes. Mr Snelgrove's wife is my housekeeper. As her husband is presently incapacitated, she asked if I might collect his winnings.'

'Garn,' exclaimed Skinner with a leer. 'Parsons collecting debts for skivvies. Whatever next? Still, at least the church is good for something I s'pose.'

Shaw looked Skinner steadily in the eye; there was a moment of silence and the bookmaker appeared slightly uncomfortable.

'Got the slip?' he asked.

Shaw handed over the small piece of paper; Skinner scrutinised it then crossed to the table and picked up some coins. He handed them to Shaw, who examined them.

'I was given to understand Mr Snelgrove only won six shillings,' said Shaw. 'This is six shillings and sixpence.'

'Lor, don't worry, I'm not overpaying him,' said Skinner with a grin. He rattled off numbers with the speed of an auctioneer. 'Sixpenny single, horse come in at 12-1, that's six bob winnings plus his tanner stake back, that's six and six goes to him.'

'I see,' said Shaw. He could not help wondering why someone with such a quick head for figures could not have found better employment. 'And the slip also?' he asked.

'Ain't used to this game, are you vicar?' said Skinner. 'I keep that. Need it for my accounting. Carbon copy to me when they place the bet, top copy for the customer, see. And when I take their slip I tear it and that tells me I paid out.' He tore the slip in half and placed the two halves together in a heap with several others on the table.

'Anything else, vicar?' asked Skinner in a bored voice. 'Like to put something on a race yourself? Or how about a little date with Judy here?'

'No thank you,' said Shaw firmly, 'but I wonder if you might furnish me with some information about a previous race.'

'Oh yes, which one? I owe Bert more money, do I?'

'No, this is merely an enquiry out of interest. A friend of mine and I were disputing when a horse named Tamsin last ran at Aintree.'

'Tamsin's only run once at Aintree,' said Skinner. 'This Wednesday. I remember that one because she was tipped as favourite but come in second to last. Had a few disappointed customers that day.'

Shaw decided to push things a little further. 'My friend *will* be pleased. You see, we found a betting slip – to be precise, half of a betting slip, one of yours perhaps, for Tamsin at Aintree, and it got us talking about the horse and disputing whether she – presumably it is a filly – had ever run before at that course.'

A dark shadow seemed to cross Skinner's face.

'Where did you find this slip?' he asked.

Shaw looked at his watch. 'Good heavens,' he said brightly. 'Is it that late already? I have taken up far too much of your valuable time. I shall be on my way.'

Skinner deftly blocked the way out of the room. He adopted a terrier-like posture of pugnacity, a habit of some small men who wish to intimidate those larger than themselves.

'I asked you a question, vicar,' he said. 'Where did you find that slip?'

'My dear sir,' said Shaw jovially. 'I fail to see that it is of any importance where your discarded litter blows. If you are so worried about the whereabouts of your betting slips perhaps you should have more care of where you conduct your business. Money-changers in the temple, as the good book tells us, tend to end up getting whipped.'

'Now see here...' said Skinner menacingly, and Shaw noticed the man's hand move towards his trouser pocket. The woman in the corner had put down her magazine and was watching them with interest. Was Skinner armed? Shaw suddenly felt his stomach clench, and wondered if Palgrave had been right to be concerned about his coming here alone. Shaw silently offered up a brief prayer for protection; it was interrupted by the ringing of the telephone bell.

'Well pick it up then!' barked Skinner, all the time fixing his eyes on Shaw.

The young woman sighed and lifted the receiver.

'Yus?' she asked. 'Haydock results,' she said in a bored voice, holding the handset out towards Skinner.

'Tell them to call back in five minutes,' he snapped, and the girl complied.

'Now,' said the bookmaker, leaning his nose forward somewhere close to the region of Shaw's chin, 'about that slip.'

'Perhaps you might ask the police,' said Shaw, looking down at a sharp angle to retain eye contact with the man. 'I understand they may find the matter of interest.'

'The police haven't...' began Skinner, and then stopped, looking round to glance at the woman behind him. Shaw sensed a sudden restraint in the man's manner, who then stepped aside to let him pass.

'All right, forget it,' said Skinner. 'I've got work to do, so clear off, will you?'

'Thank you for your time,' said Shaw. 'And goodbye Miss, ah, Judy.'

Shaw tipped his hat in the direction of the woman in the corner, who tittered into her magazine. He then swiftly exited the public house, noting with relief that his bicycle was still propped against the wall where he had left it.

Chapter Twelve

'Lord, you must have the patience of a saint, Shaw!' exclaimed Palgrave. 'I don't think I would have kept a cool head with the little tyke squaring up to me like you said. I would have punched him on the nose.'

The two men were cycling side by side along the lane which led to Palgrave's ancestral home. It was twilight on a mild, still autumnal evening, and the pair were discussing the events of the day.

'I certainly think Mr Skinner knows more than he is letting on,' said Shaw. 'We know Tamsin has only run once at Aintree, and that was on the day of the Dean's death. So the torn betting slip was not left there by someone a long time previously. '

'And it's hardly likely someone like Skinner would be in the cathedral for devotional purposes and just happened to drop it in the gallery,' said Palgrave wryly. 'I think he's our number one suspect now,' he continued. 'More shifty than Adams, from what you've told me. And besides, Adams has an alibi because he was down in the nave when Vale keeled over. Ought we to go to the police?'

Shaw recalled his meeting with Gregory and Wheatley. He felt somehow he did not yet know enough to bother them. Skinner hardly seemed likely to be an agent of a foreign power, and yet...

'Wake up, old man,' said Palgrave. 'I said ought we to

go to the police? About Skinner, I mean.'

'I think not just yet,' said Shaw. 'Let us first hear what your sister has to say. It may still be possible to keep her name out of this. If we go to the police now, she will be inevitably dragged in.'

An hour later they were relaxing in the sitting room at Mead Lodge; a frugal dinner had been prepared for them at short notice by Winnie, who had now been safely banished to the distant scullery. Shaw had noticed that Millicent seemed distracted, and he watched her carefully as he packed his pipe.

Palgrave shifted awkwardly in his armchair and cleared his throat.

'Ah...look here sis. I'm afraid we've come for a reason.'

'I didn't think it was a social call,' said Millicent. 'I can tell you've been dying to break some bad news or other to me the whole time. What is it, something to do with father's debts?'

'No,' replied Palgrave slowly. 'It's...look here. What do you know about the secret passage that leads to the King's Gallery in the cathedral?'

Shaw noticed the colour drain from Millicent's face.

'Secret passage? I've never heard of such a thing,' she replied in a neutral tone.

'Are you sure?' asked Palgrave.

'On another topic,' said Shaw, 'perhaps I ought to mention, Mrs Reynolds,' said Shaw, 'that somebody mentioned you by name in, ah, connection with the late Dean.'

This time Millicent's face flushed red.

'Just what on earth damned business of yours is that?'

'You don't deny it then?' said Palgrave bluntly. 'Carrying on with a married man.'

'How dare you come in here and accuse me of...'

'We are not accusing you of anything,' interrupted Shaw. 'But this is a very serious matter. A man has died in suspicious circumstances and you have been named in connection with him.'

'Named by whom?' asked Millicent. 'Oh, wait. I can guess. Well, all right then. I shan't try to deny it. It was perfectly honourable and decent and the man is dead now anyway, so what does it matter?'

'You admit you were lovers?' asked Palgrave; Shaw noticed the man's face was flushed with embarrassment.

'If you want to call it that,' said Millicent, angrily clicking her lighter as she attempted to light her cigarette; she waved away Shaw's offer of assistance.

'Since I seem to be facing some sort of enquiry into my moral standards,' she continued, 'I might as well be blunt. Eckhart...Mr Vale, was a perfect gentleman and kept his married vows intact, at least in physical terms. He was planning to get divorced and we were going to marry.'

'Oh yes?' asked Palgrave with a raised eyebrow.

'Don't you dare look at me with that expression,' said Millicent. 'He wasn't the sort of man to take advantage of a woman. What we had was...was pure.'

'Mrs Reynolds,' said Shaw, clearing his throat as he put down his pipe, 'your relationship with the late Dean is not so much of interest to us, as your whereabouts when he died.'

'Good God,' breathed Millicent. 'You're not accusing me of...'

'As I have said, we are not accusing anybody of anything,' said Shaw. 'But a number of things ought to be clarified.'

'But you're not a policeman,' said Millicent in disbelief. 'You're just an ordinary parson. Why should I tell you anything? And you,' she turned to her brother, 'are an interfering little…'

'Please, Mrs Reynolds,' said Shaw calmly. 'I am not a policeman, that is true. I *am* a mere ordinary parson, as you say. But there are certain things we need to discuss, unpleasant as they may be, in the hope that we do not need to involve the police at all.'

'What things?' asked Milllicent suspiciously.

'I have here a note,' said Shaw, 'obtained from the study of the late Dean, which was sent to him on the morning of his death. It is signed simply "M". Whoever M is, seemed upset that Mr Vale wished to break off relations with her. Shall I read it to you?'

'You needn't bother,' said Millicent sullenly. 'What's the other thing?'

Shaw reached into his jacket pocket and took out the folded cap, and placed it on the little occasional table in front of him. He noted that Millicent's eyes bulged.

'Yours I think,' said Shaw, turning the cap over to reveal the inner lining. 'Your name is written inside, at any rate.'

'Where…,' breathed Millicent, '…did you get that?'

'It was found in the secret passage leading to the King's Gallery. A passage you have just claimed not to have known about.'

There was a moment of silence as Millicent stared at the cap. Then she slumped forward with her head in her hands and began to sob.

A few moments later Millicent had recovered herself, while Shaw and Palgrave looked on somewhat awkwardly.

'Perhaps you ought to tell us exactly what happened on

the day of Mr Vale's death,' said Shaw gently.

'Yes, of course,' said Millicent with a sniff. 'I rode over to Midchester on Bounder and left him tied up in the usual place, a little copse between the cathedral and the river. Then when the coast was clear I used the secret door on the north wall.'

'How, may I ask, did you know about that door?' asked Shaw.

'Oh, Eckhart – Mr Vale – had known about it for a while. He'd made a study of the building when he arrived. To try to save money. You know of course he wanted it to lose its cathedral status and become a parish church.'

'I had heard something of that,' said Shaw. 'Go on.'

'He told me about it and we came up with the idea of me sitting up in the King's Gallery with him where nobody could see us. Sort of hiding in plain sight, as they way. It was silly really.'

'Damned silly if you ask me,' interjected Palgrave. 'What on earth where you thinking of?'

'I wouldn't expect a cold fish like you to understand,' said Millicent to her brother with a sudden flash of anger. 'When have *you* ever been in love?'

'Perhaps we could carry on, Mrs Reynolds?' asked Shaw. 'It was your habit to attend Evensong secretly, sitting near Mr Vale out of sight on the King's Gallery, is that correct?'

'Yes,' said Millicent. 'But the day that he…had his…accident…I didn't attend the service. He had told me it was all over. Us, I mean. That he wasn't going to divorce his wife. So I didn't come for Evensong, I came at the end to try to talk him out of it. To see if there was still a chance.'

'In heaven's name why, Millie?' asked Palgrave. 'The scandal would have been enormous. He would have been defrocked, most likely. You would have been cited as co-respondent. It would have been madness.'

'Perhaps love is a sort of madness,' said Millicent.

'Oh don't talk such rot,' said Palgrave.

'Palgrave, if I may continue?' said Shaw. 'Mrs Reynolds, I mentioned a note earlier. Did you write that note to Mr Vale telling him you would not accept his rejection?'

'I...how did you know?' asked Millicent.

'It was given to me by Mrs Vale,' said Shaw.

'I bet she relished every moment,' said Millicent angrily.

'Let us please be calm,' said Shaw. 'You arrived at the King's Gallery at the end of Evensong via the secret passage, is that correct?'

'Yes,' said Millicent.

'How, then, were you intending to have any sort of conversation with Mr Vale?' asked Shaw. 'You would have had only a few moments during the organ voluntary to talk to him. After the organ stopped playing, people might have noticed the Dean remaining in the gallery, talking to somebody.'

'I knew that,' said Millicent. 'I intended only to implore him to meet me in the secret passageway *after* Evensong. It was the only way I could approach him. There are eyes everywhere in that cathedral.'

'Very well,' said Shaw. 'You reached the top of the stairs in the secret passageway. What then?'

'When I got to the top of the stairs,' said Millicent, 'I realised it was hopeless. The organ was playing so loudly that I could never have caught Eckhart's attention from the doorway, unless I had walked right up to him and let myself be seen from the nave.'

'I didn't dare open the door more than a crack to listen,' she continued. 'Then I heard the...the scream, that was loud enough to hear over the organ. Then the music stopped and...and I knew something terrible had happened.' She pressed her fists to her mouth and squeezed her eyes shut.

'And what then?' asked Shaw gently.

'I ran and I ran and I ran,' said Millicent. 'Down that horrible staircase and out into the fresh air, and I didn't stop running until I found Bounder, and took him home at the gallop.'

'You haven't told anybody about all this?' asked Palgrave. 'The police, for example?'

'I...I didn't know what to do,' said Millicent. 'I knew it would look bad for me...and for Eckhart...if I spoke to the police. And after all, what good would it do? Eckhart is dead.'

'Dash it all sis,' exclaimed Palgrave, 'Eckhart as you call him may be dead, but did you ever stop to wonder how it happened?'

'He...he fell, of course,' said Millicent, 'like the papers are saying. That balcony rail was rotten through, you could see the worm holes in it from yards away.'

'Mrs Reynolds, did you see anyone else on the King's Gallery that day?' asked Shaw.

'How could I?' replied Millicent. 'I told you, I only opened the door a crack to listen. Why?'

'We have reason to believe,' said Palgrave, 'that Vale didn't fall. We think he may have been pushed.'

'But...that's horrible!' exclaimed Millicent. 'How can you possibly know that? Even the police are saying it was an accident.'

'Mrs Reynolds,' said Shaw, 'Please try to remain calm. I shall be blunt. You must realise how bad this looks for you. You wrote a note telling Mr Vale that you would meet him and would not accept his breaking off of your...relationship. You also left a cap with your name on it near where he fell. What else were you wearing?'

'Why, my old riding mac, of course,' said Millicent.

'The beige-coloured coat that was hanging on the hall stand as we came in?' asked Shaw.

'That's right. What has that to do with anything?'

'Mrs Reynolds,' continued Shaw, 'I was, as far as we know, the only person in the cathedral to actually see Mr Vale fall from the the King's Gallery. For an instant before he fell I chanced to glimpse a figure. All I saw of that figure was a beige-coloured coat.'

Millicent gaped. 'You *are* suggesting that I...'

'I am suggesting that you ought to speak to the police,' interrupted Shaw. 'That is all. I can accept that the last few days have been very upsetting for you but the time is now right to make an official statement, in order to be eliminated from their enquiries.'

Shaw stood up, indicating that the conversation was at an end; he saw no point in prolonging the interview. Palgrave stood also, but then Millicent raised an arm so suddenly that the empty coffee cup in front of her on the table was knocked to the floor.

'Wait,' she cried. 'I've just realised something. The cap.'

'What of it?' asked Shaw.

'That one you showed me wasn't the one I was wearing when Eckhart fell. I've two of them, similar looking but not quite the same. After the...accident...I came home in such a state I didn't notice I'd lost it. But the next day I realised I had. I looked everywhere, all along the route I'd taken with Bounder. I must have covered half of Suffolk! I then thought I must have dropped it in the secret passage and realised if I had, the police would be certain to find it. I tried desperately to retrieve it but one of the beadles nearly caught me.'

'I fail to see the relevance,' said Shaw. 'Fortunately the police are still completely unaware of the existence of the passage which is why you ought to speak to them.'

'Oh let me *explain*,' said Millicent with a flushed expression her face. 'I found the cap – the cap I'd been wearing on the night Eckhart fell – it had been wedged in a branch in the copse where I left Bounder. So I *couldn't* have left it in the secret passage that night.'

'That may be so, but unfortunately the other cap still connects you with the scene of the crime,' said Shaw.

'I see that, but I've no idea how it got there,' said Millicent. 'That particular cap had been missing for a few days before Eckhart died. I could have sworn I left it on the hall-stand by the front door, but it was gone, so I took out another one from the wardrobe.'

'Mrs Reynolds,' said Shaw. 'May I suggest you sleep on this matter? Tomorrow, shall we say in the evening, we shall all go together to the…the authorities. Kindly allow me to telephone my, ah, acquaintances in that area and I shall let you know a suitable time.'

'Very well,' said Millicent, dabbing her eyes with a handkerchief. 'You're right of course. I shall sleep on it.'

'I say Shaw,' said Palgrave as the two men each drank a cup of cocoa to warm themselves after the chilly night cycle home, 'you were a bit harsh on old Milly. You don't really think she pushed Vale off that gallery, do you?'

'I had to be rather firm with her,' said Shaw carefully, 'as until I had spoken to her I was not sure what to think about her involvement. But now…I am reasonably certain she is telling the truth and had no involvement in Mr Vale's death.'

'*Reasonably* certain?' asked Palgrave. 'Look here, I know

194

she's my own sister and I think the world of her, but one never really knows, does one? For instance until this evening I would never have thought her capable of a love affair with a married man.'

'There is something I have overlooked,' said Shaw. 'Some detail.'

'You mean in what Milly said?' asked Palgrave. 'She sounded convincingly innocent to me.'

'Not in what your sister said, no,' said Shaw. 'It was something else.'

'You mean, if sis didn't drop that cap in the staircase, how did it get there?'

'Yes, there is that,' replied Shaw slowly, 'but there is something else... I need to recall this before we speak to the police tomorrow.'

'This person you saw in a raincoat on the gallery,' said Palgrave. 'You don't think that was Milly, do you?'

'No,' said Shaw.

'Who then? Skinner? We know that was one of his betting slips we found up there. I noted you didn't mention that to Milly.'

'It is always best not to tell *everything* one knows,' said Shaw cryptically. 'And yes, I do think Skinner may be involved somehow. But there is something more going on. Something I have overlooked. I must *think*.'

'Your brain's overheating, old man,' said Palgrave. He stood up and yawned. 'I'm bushed, as the Americans say. Get a good night's sleep, we'll need it if we're to spend all tomorrow in some police station making statements. I say, do you think we ought to go together? To the police, I mean?'

'Most definitely,' said Shaw. 'Your sister will need all the help she can get.'

'Right you are,' said Palgrave. 'I've rehearsals tomorrow

morning for Vale's funeral – won't that be jolly – and I'm playing at Evensong but after that I'm free. Or will that be too late?'

'That will give me time to gather my thoughts during the day and summarise what is to be said to the police,' said Shaw. It would also, he decided, give him time to speak to Gregory and Wheatley on the telephone about what he had found out.

'Very well,' said Shaw, and he bade goodnight to Palgrave and made his way up to the little bedroom. He knew it was his duty to speak to Gregory and Wheatley about what he had found out, but he was wary of what they would do to Millicent with such circumstantial evidence against her.

As he got into bed he again felt that nagging sensation in the back of his mind that he was missing something. Fortunately, he fell into a deep slumber the moment he closed his eyes.

It was the last day of the conference, and Shaw felt he ought to make an appearance. He sat through the morning lecture, though he was unable to pay much attention to the proceedings.

Over and over again in his mind's eye he saw the faded plans of the King's Gallery. So much so, that when it came time for luncheon, he walked briskly back to Palgrave's house and examined the ancient ledger while he ate the cold collation left for him by Mrs Snelgrove, trying to avoid getting any crumbs on the book.

He disliked reading and eating at the same time but he was determined to stop the image of the plans constantly unrolling themselves in his brain, as if projected by some malevolent mental cinematography.

No inspiration came, and Shaw returned to Diocesan House for the final afternoon lectures. There was to be a farewell dinner for the delegates that evening, but Shaw excused himself, knowing he would likely be spending the evening in a police station.

At teatime, he returned to Palgrave's house, but finding Mrs Snelgrove nowhere in evidence to prepare that particular refreshment, he contented himself with a pipeful of tobacco instead. He picked up the ledger again and traced his finger along the elevation which showed the panelling at the rear of the gallery, and the empty space of the vaulted ceiling above. Again no inspiration came. He knocked out his pipe into the empty grate, and got up to go; thinking that perhaps a walk would do him good.

The door-knocker rattled; Shaw opened the door to see a Post Office Telegrams boy holding the handlebars of his bicycle in one hand and a slip of paper in the other.

'Name of Shaw?' asked the boy.

Shaw assented.

'Telegram for you sir,' said the boy brightly, and held out the slip of paper.

Shaw took the missive and tipped the boy sixpence; the youth gave a smart salute and pedalled away rapidly down the Close.

Shaw frowned; a telegram generally meant bad news. Was something wrong at home? He felt a sudden pang of guilt at leaving his wife alone, and quickly opened the envelope. He frowned again when he read the message:

MUST SPEAK WITH YOU. MEET ON ROOF 6.00 PM USE PASSAGE. COME ALONE TELL NO-ONE. MILLICENT REYNOLDS

197

Shaw spent the next two hours smoking another two pipes and pondering what to do as he sat alone in the little house. He climbed the stairs to the little bedroom and knelt to pray by the bed, but felt little comfort in it. Had he been right to suspect Millicent? Was she about to confess to some involvement in Vale's death? Or perhaps tell him something that she had felt unable to say in front of her brother?

Shaw also pondered the instruction that he must tell nobody. Could he risk a meeting, on a cathedral roof of all places, with somebody who might have recently committed murder by pushing a man off a balcony? Would it be breaching trust if he were to tell Palgrave? He decided it would be. He must face this alone.

He thought back to the first murder case he had been involved in; that time he had, extremely rashly, confronted a killer, and nearly been killed himself. He could not risk that again; it would not be fair to his wife, his family or his parishioners. And yet…he could not ignore that telegram.

The bell for Evensong started; the ancient sound drifting through the partly opened casement. It would soon be six o'clock and if he was to make it to the roof in time he would have to leave now. He had to go, but there was something he must do first.

With trembling hands Shaw opened the drawer of the dresser that contained Palgrave's mementoes, and examined the contents.

Ten minutes later Shaw was striding across Cathedral Green towards the concealed entrance on the north wall. As the tolling of the large, deep tenor bell increased in speed, indicating the service was soon to begin, he looked up at the tower and then to the roof.

The roof! Suddenly, he realised what he had been struggling to remember. The nagging, formless thought at the back of his mind became whole and clear. He stopped dead in his tracks and looked at his wrist-watch. Seven minutes. He had been told not to tell anyone of the appointment, but who would find out at this late stage? He had to risk it.

He turned around and walked briskly back to the Cathedral Close and found again the telephone kiosk he had used before. His heart sank as he saw that it was occupied by a middle aged woman in a headscarf. How long would she be? Dare he tap on the glass, and tell her it was an emergency? He did not have to, as a few moments later she exited the box.

He entered, fumbled in his pocket for the card that Wheatley had given him, and asked the operator for the London number shown on it. Realising he did not have sufficient coins for such an expensive call, he threw caution to the winds and asked for the charges to be reversed.

'The trunk line to London is extremely busy, caller,' said the efficient female voice at the telephone exchange. 'You may have to wait some time. Kindly replace your receiver and you will be called back.'

'How long?' exclaimed Shaw, looking at his watch again.

'Kindly replace your receiver.'

Shaw realised it was hopeless to quibble with the woman, and followed her instructions. For what seemed like an age he drummed his fingers on the glass of the kiosk, and then snatched up the receiver the instant the bell rang.

'I have your London number now caller,' said the

woman. There was a moment of silence and a crackle, and then another woman's voice; this one clipped and military sounding.

'Universal Imports. Which extension please?'

Shaw squinted at the card. 'I don't know. I want Major Wheatley.'

'Who?'

'Major Wheatley. Please hurry, it's urgent.'

'I'm sorry, there is nobody of that name here.'

'But there must be. My name is Shaw. Major Wheatley told me…'

'I'm sorry,' repeated the woman more firmly, 'there is nobody of that name here. Goodbye.'

'Wait!' shouted Shaw, after a sudden burst of mental energy stimulated his memory. 'Sands! I wish to speak to Mr Sands!'

There was silence. Had the connection been lost? Shaw sighed audibly with relief when he heard the woman's voice again on the line.

'One moment sir.'

The line went dead and Shaw wondered if he had been disconnected again, but then another voice, this time a young male patrician drawl, came through the earpiece.

'Major Wheatley's office. Duty officer speaking.'

'I need to speak to him urgently, where is he?' gasped Shaw with mounting frustration.

'I'm sorry, but the Major is in conference.'

'I must…' began Shaw, but then he realised the bell for Evensong had stopped.

'There's no time,' he continued rapidly. 'Tell him Reverend Shaw requires urgent assistance at the cathedral. He will understand.'

Then he slammed down the receiver and raced across Cathedral Green.

A few moments later he had found the entrance to the secret passage; he groped his way by match-light up the stairs. As he passed the door to the King's Gallery he heard the sound of the opening hymn for Evensong drifting upwards, then he emerged from the wooden trap door which led to the roof.

Evening sunlight tinged the vast expanse of the leaded roof with an orange glow, and a light breeze blew across from the north, hinting at approaching autumn. Shaw looked at the figure standing a few feet away from him, and called out.

'Mrs Vale! Good evening!'

The woman looked at him with an expression of surprise. 'Why, Mr Shaw! What on earth are you doing up here?'

'I might well ask you the same question,' said Shaw.

There was a moment of silence.

'I...it's all rather peculiar,' said Mrs Vale. 'I received a telegram telling me to meet someone here.'

'Let me guess,' said Shaw. 'The telegram was from Millicent Reynolds.'

'How on earth did you know?'

'Because I received one also.'

'But I don't understand,' said Mrs Vale. 'She told me to come alone, and tell no-one. Why would she tell you also?'

'I think you know, Mrs Vale,' said Shaw, stepping closer to her. 'Please, let us not insult each other's intelligence any longer.'

'What do you mean, Mr Shaw? This is all highly irregular.'

'How did you get up to the roof, Mrs Vale?' asked Shaw lightly.

'I came through the door on the steeple, of course. Eckhart showed it to me once, and said it was always kept unlocked.'

'And yet you have not asked me how I came up here,' said Shaw.

'Why, I suppose, by, the, ah, secret passage that we discussed on our previous meeting.'

'That is my point, Mrs Vale,' said Shaw. 'You see, when we last met, you claimed never to have been in the secret staircase; all that you knew of it was from the plans in the ledger book.'

'That is correct,' said Mrs Vale. 'But I don't see what that has to do with anything.'

'You mentioned that the secret passage served the King's Gallery *and* the roof,' said Shaw. 'But the plans in the ledger book do not show the passage to the roof. They only mention a door to the churchyard. That suggested to me you *had* used the secret passage.'

'I…my late husband must have told me about it,' said Mrs Vale. 'Yes, yes, that's right, he did.'

'I doubt it, Mrs Vale,' said Shaw. 'You see, you also mentioned during our meeting that you did not know the location of the secret door, because you were unable to see the north wall of the cathedral from your window. If you did not know the location of the door, how did you know it was on the north wall?'

'I…I simply assumed, as that was the only wall out of sight from the house, that it must be there,' ventured Mrs Vale.

'I think not,' replied Shaw.. 'In fact, I think you know far more about your husband's death than you are letting on.'

'This is preposterous,' spluttered Mrs Vale. 'Who are you to…just exactly what do you know? Or rather, *think* you know?'

'I think,' said Shaw gently, 'that you had some considerable disagreement with your late husband over money. Gambling debts, to be specific.'

'How could you possibly know that?'

'When you allowed me to search through Mr Vale's desk, I found a letter from a firm of solicitors offering to discuss the matter.'

'You had no business to rummage through...'

'You gave me permission, Mrs Vale,' interrupted Shaw. 'I assume you checked his papers first for any such incriminating material, but failed to find that particular letter.'

'How do you know they are gambling debts? If indeed they are?'

'Because a certain person connected with the horse-racing fraternity has been seen loitering in the cathedral precincts, particularly in the area of the Dean's house. A Mr Skinner.'

Shaw watched Mrs Vale's face carefully. Her eyes registered surprise momentarily, before the mask of bland affrontery returned.

'You admitted yourself,' said Shaw, 'that you knew of the passage's existence. I think that you somehow used it to confront your husband during Evensong. Perhaps about his alleged adultery, or perhaps over your debts. Did he refuse to pay them? There was an attempt to avoid a scene; there was an altercation, and he fell. It was most likely an accident, was it not? If you come with me to the authorities now, the whole matter can be cleared up.'

'Ridiculous,' said Mrs Vale.

'There is more,' said Shaw. 'I was the only person, as far as we know, in the nave, to see your late husband falling from the King's Gallery. But I also saw another figure on the Gallery, albeit very briefly. A figure in a beige raincoat.'

Mrs Vale swallowed, but said nothing.

'I believe that figure was your bookmaker friend, Mr

Skinner,' said Shaw. 'I wonder if it was he to whom you owed money, and he was somehow involved in the confrontation with your husband?'

'How on earth could you believe such a thing?' asked Mrs Vale. 'What proof do you have?'

'No real proof, I admit,' said Shaw. 'Only half a betting slip written by him, which was found on the King's Gallery. And another thing. A cap which was found in the secret passage. A cap belonging to Mrs Reynolds.'

'Well that explains it then!' said Mrs Vale triumphantly. 'It is she you ought to be interrogating, not I. She wears a beige raincoat and cap. I saw her on more than one occasion, skulking around, presumably hoping to make some sort of assignation.'

'I have spoken to Mrs Reynolds,' said Shaw, 'and I am reasonably certain she could not have dropped that cap there.'

'Well then how did it get there?' asked Mrs Vale.

'I believe you placed it there,' said Shaw. 'In the hope that it would be found by the authorities and a connection made between Mrs Reynolds and the death of your husband.'

'In what way could I have done that?' expostulated Mrs Vale.

'I believe you stole the cap from Mrs Reynold's house a few days previous to your husband's death.'

'And just how would I do that?' spluttered Mrs Vale. 'I've never visited her house in my life.'

'I think,' said Shaw slowly, 'that you stole that cap because you were planning to murder your husband.'

Mrs Vale's eyes narrowed. Her bluster seemed to be at an end.

'A few moments ago you said you were sure it was an accident,' she said. 'And now you say it's murder. Kindly make up your mind just what it is I am supposed to be guilty of.'

'I changed my mind just now,' said Shaw, 'because you said you have never visited Mrs Reynold's house. That was a foolish mistake. You *have* visited, on more than one occasion. On the pretext of charity work. It would have been quite possible to steal Mrs Reynold's cap from the hat-stand in her hallway.'

'Well if she turns up, we can ask her, can't we?' said Mrs Vale. 'Although why on earth she wanted to meet us up here…'

'I do not believe Mrs Reynolds sent those telegrams,' said Shaw. 'I believe *you* did. It was a ruse to get me up here. For what reason, I know not, but the time has come to end this.'

Cold rage now crept into Mrs Vale's voice, and she walked a pace closer to Shaw across the leaded roof.

'Very well,' said Mrs Vale. 'If you know all this, assuming it is true, just what do you intend to do? None of it would stand up in a court of law.'

'I am neither lawyer nor policeman,' said Shaw. 'I do know, however, that there is sufficient circumstantial evidence in my possession to oblige me to speak to the police about what I suspect, and I shall do so unless you are able to somehow convince me otherwise. Now, will you kindly come with me to the police station?'

There was a moment of silence; all that could be heard was the gentle sighing of the wind. But then, there was the sound of movement from behind one of the buttresses nearby, as if a bird or small rodent had scurried past. Shaw turned to the direction of the noise, and called out.

'I assume that is you, Mr Skinner. You can come out now.'

Chapter Thirteen

'Do as he says, Len,' said Mrs Vale.

Skinner emerged from behind the stack of masonry; he was clad in his usual cap and raincoat and had his hands in his coat pockets.

He spat on the roof in front of Shaw and then looked up. 'Clever bleeder, ain't you?' he said. 'Think you've got it all worked out. That's a laugh.'

'I think nothing of the kind,' said Shaw firmly. 'But I remain unconvinced of the complete lack of involvement of yourself and Mrs Vale in this matter, and must therefore insist that you accompany me to the police station.'

Skinner laughed; a staccato mockery which was devoid of humour.

'I've never walked into a police station of my own free will and I'm not about to start,' he snarled.

'Then you leave me no alternative but to report this matter myself,' said Shaw, and turned towards the trap door.

Skinner stepped forward and blocked the entrance to the door. 'You're not going anywhere, vicar,' he snapped.

'Mrs Vale,' said Shaw, 'if this man has intimidated you in some way, then...'

'Oh be quiet,' said Mrs Vale wearily. 'Len hasn't intimidated me. In fact he's been very helpful. You see, we came to a little agreement. I offered to pay the gambling debts I owed him out of my husband's inheritance, plus something for a little job I wanted him to do. He hasn't got it yet, but once the will comes through he shall.'

'A thousand quid,' said Skinner. 'Not bad for a job I didn't end up doing.'

'A...job?' asked Shaw.

'I asked Mr Skinner to deal with my husband,' said Mrs Vale blandly. 'In a Cathedral Close one does not meet with many hired killers. But I knew something of Mr Skinner's reputation, and he agreed readily to the plan.'

'Which was...? asked Shaw. He forced himself to stay calm, and his eyes scanned the roof briefly for an escape route. The passage door was blocked, but could he make it to the tower door before Skinner, he wondered?

'It wasn't strictly speaking a murder plot,' said Mrs Vale. 'It was blackmail, I suppose. Eckhart refused to pay my debts to Mr Skinner, and was threatening a divorce, trying to cut me off without a penny. I knew he wouldn't risk such a scandal, and so I called his bluff. He still refused to pay. The only way I could think of was to threaten to stand up in church and tell everyone just what he was doing – meeting another woman in secret. Yet again, he refused to give in – I suppose I should have admired his fortitude – but instead, Mr Skinner and I decided to show him we were serious by confronting him during the voluntary at Evensong.'

'I even had a tart lined up downstairs,' said Skinner. 'We didn't want to bring her up, just in case things had to get nasty...but she was all ready to swear blind her and the Dean were sweethearts, right in front of everyone in church,' he added with a chuckle. 'Never needed to call her up in the end though, did I?'

'What...what happened then?' asked Shaw.

'Eckhart still refused to be cowed,' said Mrs Vale. 'So

Len had to show him he "meant business" as they say.'

Skinner grinned and produced his open razor from his pocket, and waved it slowly as he stepped closer to Shaw.

'And so he fell,' said Shaw. 'That is not murder, Mrs Vale. It is still an accident, or manslaughter at most. If you go to the police now…'

'Oh it was no accident,' said Mrs Vale. 'It was Len that was supposed to do the deed. I always thought Eckhart might fight back, which is why I stole that woman's cap and planted it in advance, as a way of throwing the police off Len's trail.'

'But it didn't matter 'cos the police thought it was an accident,' said Skinner. 'So looks like Mrs Dean here got off scot free, until you came along that is.'

'Mrs Vale…you mean…?' said Shaw.

'Yes Mr Shaw,' said Mrs Vale. 'Mr Skinner only *threatened* to attack my husband. Yet it was *me* who pushed him over.'

'But…why?' asked Shaw.

'That man,' said Mrs Vale, 'humiliated me constantly during the course of our marriage. With his dalliances with other women, and his ridiculous posturing at being a socialist despite coming from the one of the wealthiest families in England. And then refusing to pay my debts, which were a pittance compared to his fortune. He made my life hell.'

'It was a momentary lapse of reason,' said Shaw.

'No,' said Mrs Vale, shaking her head. 'I was reasonably certain either myself or Len would end up killing him. That was why I placed the cap in the secret passage. Mr Skinner obliged by placing a couple of blonde hairs from one of his…lady friends…inside, to further incriminate Mrs Reynolds. It's a pity that trick didn't work, as we could have killed two birds with one stone, as they say.'

'Why...are you telling me all this?' asked Shaw. And yet, deep down, he knew why.

'I had to find out what you knew,' said Mrs Vale. 'That's why I pretended to be upset with the police thinking Eckhart's death was an accident, and asked you to investigate. I wanted to keep you under observation as I knew you had already started to become interested. But then you visited Mr Skinner here.'

'I was a bit of a silly boy,' said Skinner, still holding up his razor. 'Dropped one of my betting slips in all the fuss on that balcony. But you were a silly boy too. When you asked about that race I knew something rum was going on.'

'And so Mr Skinner telephoned me,' said Mrs Vale, 'and warned me about you. I decided the time had come to find out exactly what you knew, and if it was too much, to, ah, deal with you.'

'May I assume,' said Shaw, 'that you have come to the conclusion that I am to be "dealt with"?'

'I am not a cold blooded killer,' said Mrs Vale, 'but Mr Skinner has some expertise in that area. We agreed a fee previously for the...despatch...of my late husband, which was not required, but the money will go to him instead for dealing with *you*. You are to suffer a mysterious fall from this roof, and will be found with the telegram from Mrs Reynolds in your pocket, which ought to be of interest to the police.'

'That would be most foolish,' said Shaw. 'The police will ask questions, and inevitably draw similar conclusions as I did. Mr Palgrave, the organist, knows something of my theories regarding this case also.'

Shaw then wished he had not mentioned Palgrave, as Mrs Vale merely smiled. 'If necessary, Mr Palgrave will be dealt with also. But in all probability it will not matter as I intend to disappear abroad if necessary, as will Mr Skinner. If some guilt can be conferred on the Reynolds woman, then so much the better.'

'And if I refuse to have this mysterious accident?' asked Shaw. 'Would you have a murder on your conscience, Mr Skinner?'

'I don't think I've got one of them conscience things,' said Skinner, stepping dangerously close to Shaw. He stepped back to avoid the razor which the man waved in front of his face, and realised his route to the tower was cut off by another buttress. He glanced behind and saw the low wall of the roof just a few feet away.

'I've got ways of persuading people to do what I want, see,' continued Skinner, with a cold glint in his eyes, 'and it doesn't bother me what those ways are. Do you know, the first time I killed a man I was only 19? 19 years of age, over in France. Just a kiddie, when you think about it.

'I found a Jerry in a shell hole. Couldn't have been more than sixteen years old. Cowering he was, with his hands above his head. "*Kamerad, kamerad*" he kept whining. I soon stopped his "*kamerad*" by bashing his head in with my rifle butt. Even got a clap on the back from my captain for it. "Well done Skinner", he says. "Well done," like I'd just polished his boots for him.

'Now, that boy never done me any harm, but I never thought anything of it, nor with the others since. And I reckon if it's all right to kill a man in cold blood because the army tells me it's my job, then it's all right to do it any old time. So what makes you think I'll care tuppence about tipping you over the edge of this wall, 'specially if there's a thousand quid in it for me?'

Skinner lunged forward and Shaw recoiled, reaching back to steady himself against the wall. As the man raised his hand to strike with his razor, Shaw reached under his coat and pulled out Palgrave's service revolver.

'That's far enough,' said Shaw firmly, pointing the weapon at Skinner's midriff.

Skinner looked down and then recoiled, struggling to retain his balance. His razor clattered to the floor, and Shaw deftly kicked it away. Skinner then stood up straight, raised his hands, and uttered a foul expletive.

'A vicar with a gun, now I've seen it all,' he added.

'Kindly stay where you are,' said Shaw. 'You also, Mrs Vale,' he added, pointing the barrel momentarily at the woman, who had jumped behind Skinner when she saw the pistol.

'Know how to use that, do you?' asked Skinner, his hands still raised heavenward.

'Sufficiently well,' said Shaw, 'but I will at least grant more mercy to you than you granted that boy in France, as long as you keep your hands raised.'

'You haven't got a clue, mate,' said Skinner with a chuckle. 'That gun's not cocked. Heavy action, them Webley hammers. Might need both hands. By the time you manage it, I'll have it away from you.'

Shaw fumbled for the hammer but, as promised, Skinner grabbed the pistol and wrenched it out of his hand. With a triumphant laugh he raised the weapon, cocked it deftly and fired at Shaw's chest.

There was an enormous explosion and Shaw fell backwards against the low wall; he saw what seemed to be hundreds of birds rising into the air from the cathedral roof as an exultant 'Amen' rose upwards from the choir below him in the nave. Was this death?

Then he heard a man's scream. Skinner had staggered backwards. His shirt-front smouldered, and he clutched two bloodied, blackened hands to his face, which had become similarly discoloured.

'I'm blind!' he yelled hoarsely, and fell to the floor, writhing in agony.

The gun, thought Shaw. Something had happened to the gun; it lay beside Skinner, the revolving chamber contorted into shards of smoking metal.

Mrs Vale yelled with rage and launched herself at Shaw; although a slight woman, the impact was sufficient to knock him over the low wall of the roof. His feet scrabbled against the ancient stones; he realised he was only holding on by his arms. He looked down and his stomach lurched as he realised just how high up he was. Figures, the size of lead soldiers, were already gathering on the Green, presumably attracted by the noise from the roof; there were indistinct yells and then the shrill, urgent sound of a police whistle.

With a gasp of relief, Shaw felt his feet find purchase on the tiniest of ledges. He grasped at the stone balustrade but felt it move almost imperceptibly, like a loose tooth, as the ancient mortar crumbled under the strain. Then he felt a searing pain in his hands and arms as he struggled to hold on. Mrs Vale was kicking and punching him.

'Let...go...!' she hissed.

'It's over!' yelled Shaw. 'For God's sake, stop.'

Ignoring him, she aimed a terrific kick at his right hand, but misjudged it, her neat little brogue connecting with the stone balustrade instead. In that instant, the crumbling masonry gave way and Mrs Vale, carried by her own momentum, fell almost gracefully over the balustrade.

Shaw looked down, and later, was convinced he had heard her say 'forgive me', before her final screams merged with those of the crowd gathered a hundred feet below.

Then, just as the last of his strength ebbed away, he felt strong arms pulling him upwards on to the roof.

It was the day after the dramatic events on the cathedral roof, and Shaw, although still wincing with pain, had been cleared of any serious injury. Wheatley and Gregory had satisfied themselves that no sinister agents of a foreign power were involved in the Dean's death, and had returned the matter entirely into the hands of the local police, with an admonishment to be less quick in dismissing suspicious deaths as mere accidents.

'Well done, Mr Shaw,' said Major Wheatley, as he and the Superintendent were shown to the front door of Palgrave's house. Shaw could not help feeling he had somehow passed some sort of test.

'We'll leave the lovely ladies to fuss over you,' he added, tipping his hat to Millicent and Mrs Snelgrove who were anxious to apply various minor medications and cure-alls to Shaw's person, of the type used when no major physical damage has been suffered.

'Goodbye gentlemen,' said Shaw. 'I am sorry I could not be of more use.'

'Oh you were useful enough,' said Gregory. 'But in future don't play around with guns, eh? Leave that to the professionals.'

Then the two mysterious men were gone, whisked away by a large dark car which had appeared from nowhere.

'What on earth were you talking with those two about up in your bedroom?' asked Palgrave. 'I thought the police spoke to you yesterday. They *were* coppers?'

'They are…connected with the case,' said Shaw carefully. 'A few loose ends to be tied up.'

'May we know what they are?' asked Palgrave.

'Doubtless you will find out yourself when the case comes to trial,' said Shaw carefully, 'but the item of most interest discussed was that Skinner says he can produce a woman friend who will support his claim that he did not plan to kill Vale. The police are looking for her now.'

'Woman friend, eh?' said Palgrave. 'Someone he was living off, most likely. I don't see how that will help. Isn't there something called, what is it, "joint enterprise"? And he tried to kill you, as well. He's for the long drop, I expect.'

'Most probably,' said Shaw sadly. 'From what the police have told me. It seems he was suspected of involvement in other killings previously, but nothing was proven. The police are to reopen several cases.'

'Well, I know one thing,' said Palgrave. 'That fellow just now was right about that revolver. What on earth did you think you were doing? Didn't I tell you it was faulty?'

'You never even mentioned its existence,' said Shaw. 'I noticed it when you showed me the regimental photograph.'

'I could have sworn blind I told you about it,' said Palgrave. 'That was the one that jammed on the range just after I arrived in France. The armourer said it was some rare fault – a bubble in the steel, one in a million chance, and if I'd fired it again it might explode. Yes – I did tell you about it, when we were looking at the staff photo.'

'No,' corrected Shaw. 'You merely told me that you had not yet been issued with your revolver when that photograph was taken.'

'Ah, apologies, old man. You're right, of course. I had to wait a day or two to get the new one, and could hardly have the old wreck smouldering away in my Sam Browne. I was supposed to hand the old one in, but then we had the big push up the line, and the new QM down from Brigade refused to take it because I didn't have the right chit. You know what the army's like. In the end I decided to keep it, and the remaining rounds, as a sort of, what do you call it, *memento mori.'*

'It was entirely my fault,' said Shaw. 'I should have remembered that "they that live by the sword, shall die by the sword". Mr Skinner is proof of that.'

'Don't be ridiculous,' said Millicent, as she checked a bandage on Shaw's hand. 'You're alive and Skinner's dead, or soon will be, when the law runs its course. It was an entirely reasonable thing to go armed when you thought you might be confronting a killer. It's Tom's damned-fool fault for leaving that broken gun where anyone could find it.'

'I am indebted to your brother for pulling me safely from the roof,' said Shaw. 'I feel in no mood to quibble over the responsibility for faulty firearms.'

'I knew something was up when I heard thudding on the roof during the Prayers of Intercession,' said Palgrave. 'The organ loft's pretty close. And when I heard that bang, well I knew something *really* was up. I've no idea who called the police, though.'

'That was, ah, me,' said Shaw. 'I suspected something was not quite right about the telegram asking me to meet with Mrs Reynolds on the roof, and telephoned a warning to, ah, the authorities.'

'That Mrs Vale was clever,' said Millicent. 'She sent me a telegram as well – some cock and bull story about a sick relative in Ipswich. When I got to the hospital they didn't know anything about it.'

'That was, presumably, to ensure that you would not turn up by chance at the cathedral, and spoil her plans,' said Shaw.

'Well,' said Palgrave, 'I hope Angry Adams can forgive me for running up to the roof before the end of the last hymn.'

'Dr Adams has been very kind,' said Shaw. 'I am sorry we ever suspected he might be involved in the death of the Dean in some way.'

'At least he can sell off the cathedral land now, and get his building scheme up and running,' said Palgrave. 'Oh, that reminds me,' he added. 'In all the fuss I forgot to mention it. While we were all waiting interminably to speak to the police last night, I spoke with our Dr Adams and it seems he has an idea which might save Mead Lodge.'

'Really?' asked Millicent.

'Yes, really,' said Palgrave. 'He wants to organise more of these conferences, as often as possible – they bring in a lot of money, it seems – but they need more rooms for the delegates. There isn't anything suitable in town, but he wondered if we'd be interested in having, well, "paying guests" at the Lodge. The rates would be quite good, and they would lay on some sort of charabanc to ferry them back and forth.'

Millicent clapped her hands together. 'We've got ten spare bedrooms,' she exclaimed. 'Why, even if they pay, say, just five shillings a night, that's two pounds ten a night. If they stayed for a week...'

'Steady on sis,' said Palgrave. 'Love of money is the root of all evil. But I agree, it would rather solve our immediate problems.'

'And there was me with ridiculous romantic fantasies of marrying a wealthy man, who would whisk me away like some fairy tale,' said Millicent. 'Oh dear, I *have* been awfully stupid, haven't I?'

There was an awkward pause, which Mrs Snelgrove broke as she applied a damp flannel to Shaw's forehead.

'I don't know about any o' that, but I've nursed enough people to know this gentleman needs rest,' she said primly.

'Really Mrs S, I am perfectly all right,' said Shaw, as he struggled to evade her ministrations.

'Now you just sit and rest,' admonished the servant. 'I don't know about no building schemes, or love affairs, or charabancs, but that Len Skinner got what he deserved if you ask me. And if you hadn't a done it, Mr Shaw, another would have. Nasty piece of work. They say he might be blinded in one eye. Well, an eye for an eye, the Bible says. That's justice.'

'Singing like a canary, too, as they say in the American films, eh Shaw?' asked Palgrave.

'He is, apparently, corroborating everything I told the police,' said Shaw. 'Of course, it is in his interest for Mrs Vale to be blamed *post-mortem* for killing the Dean. But the other killings he has been implicated in will come to light.'

'I hope he hangs,' said Mrs Snelgrove firmly. 'And if that ain't a Christian thing to say, so be it. By the way, did he give you that money he owes my Bert? That is, Mr Snelgrove?'

Shaw smiled and handed the six shillings and sixpence to her. 'Mr Skinner will at least have time to repent,' he said. 'but did Mrs Vale have time? "Betwixt the stirrup and the ground..."'

'Eh?' asked Mrs Snelgrove. 'Stirrup? You're not getting on a horse in your condition!'

'I think he's quoting poetry,' said Millicent, 'but that reminds me, I've left Bounder on the green. He'll be wanting a feed soon, so I'll get back home.'

Shaw and Palgrave stood up as Millicent moved to the door.

'I ought to go soon also,' said Shaw, ''no, Mrs S, I insist. I am due back in Lower Addenham for service tomorrow, and my wife will doubtless already have heard all sorts of rumours about my condition which I must put to rest. It was all I could do to prevent her coming here when we spoke on the telephone earlier.'

'All right, old man,' said Palgrave. 'But have a bit more rest first, and let me put your bicycle on the train for you. And don't go worrying about Mrs Vale's soul. If she didn't, why should you?'

'Perhaps you are right,' mused Shaw. 'That is out of my hands now.'

Palgrave frowned. 'It was never in them, old boy.'

The following day was Sunday, and Shaw by now had returned home. He delegated the taking of Matins to his curate, but by late afternoon was feeling well enough to preside at Evensong. A great sense of peace descended on him as he stood in the chancel, facing the handful of worshippers in the nave. He came to the familiar responses:

'Give peace in our time, O Lord: Because there is none other that fighteth for us, but only thou, O God.'

He nodded to himself, and noted a look of concern on his wife's face as she sat watching from the front pew. He recited the Collects with professional ease, but his mind was elsewhere.

Palgrave's idea, that he, Shaw, had somehow been chosen to uncover the truth about Vale's death seemed vain, almost self indulgent. It was only God that fought for us, and we were simply His servants.

And yet...by some strange process beyond his comprehension, he had been called upon to fight, in a way that could not be explained by mere chance. How could it possibly keep happening, he reflected, unless it *were* ordained in some way? He shook his head to rid himself of idle speculation, and launched lustily into the final hymn.

It was *God Moves In A Mysterious Way.*

Some eighty miles away, sonorous bells were ringing to announce another Evensong at the vast edifice known as Westminster Abbey. A few hundred yards away from that, in an equally vast, but entirely secular edifice, the commandment to honour the Sabbath day and keep it holy was being breached, as it always was.

In this labyrinthine building there was no Sunday calm as in other offices. Efficient secretaries, working their one weekend in four, pushed trollies decked with files along linoleum-covered corridors, past men in various different uniforms. Telephones trilled; typewriters chattered, and mimeograph machines rattled in a never-ending mechanical chorus.

In a department whose existence was all but unknown to those outside it except a handful of senior Cabinet members, one particular room had the words 'A.J. Wheatley, Maj.' emblazoned on the frosted glass door. The room's incumbent had now left to enjoy the remainder of his day off on a golf course deep in Middlesex, but he had given a report to the secretary to file, with the word 'Secret' stamped on the cover.

The report concerned various activities and personages in a place entitled, somewhat confusingly, 'East Anglia and South East Midlands Command Division (West)'. Under the heading 'Persons of particular note in this Division' one entry stood out as being the only civilian listed; the others all having military ranks. His details were as follows:

'Shaw, Reverend Lucian. Educated Mellingborough School and Newton College, Cambridge. Suffolk Regiment

Chaplaincy, 1914-1919. Has assisted police in several cases, two involving national security. Service record: impeccable. Political views: conventional. Compromising activities: none known. '

The last line was typed in red ink and underlined: 'Recommend this department approach him for assistance in future cases.'

The secretary slammed the filing cabinet door shut, left the room, and clattered her trolley briskly down the corridor to the next office, as the bells for Evensong finally stopped.

Other books by Hugh Morrison

A Third Class Murder (Reverend Shaw's first case)
An antiques dealer is found robbed and murdered in a third class train compartment on a remote Suffolk branch line. The Reverend Lucian Shaw, who was travelling on the same train, is concerned that the police have arrested the wrong man, and begins an investigation of his own.

The King is Dead
An exiled Balkan king is shot dead in his secluded mansion following a meeting with the local vicar, Reverend Shaw. Shaw believes that the culprit is closer than the police think, and before long is on the trail of a desperate killer who will stop at nothing.

The Wooden Witness
After finding the battered corpse of a spiritualist medium at an archaeological site on the Suffolk coast, Reverend Shaw is thrust into a dark and deadly mystery involving ancient texts and modern technology.

Death on the Night Train
Reverend Shaw is called to the deathbed of an elderly relative in Scotland by an anonymous telegram. Soon he becomes embroiled in a fiendish conspiracy which reaches to the highest levels of the British establishment.

Murder in Act Three
When a cast member is killed during an amateur dramatics performance in the village hall, everyone thinks it was just a terrible accident. Everyone, that is, except Reverend Shaw. But can he find out the truth before the killer strikes again?

Published by Montpelier Publishing
www.hughmorrisonbooks.com
Order from Amazon or via your local bookshop.